SUNS OF TULANNI

The Dark Hill Book II

KRISTAL LEE

Copyright © 2020
KRISTAL LEE
SUNS OF TULANNI
The Dark Hill Book II
All rights reserved.

No part of this publication may be reproduced, distributed, or transmitted in any form or by any means, including photocopying, recording, or other electronic or mechanical methods, without the prior written permission of the publisher, except in the case of brief quotations embodied in critical reviews and certain other non-commercial uses permitted by copyright law.

KRISTAL LEE

Printed in the United States of America
First Printing 2021
First Edition 2021

10 9 8 7 6 5 4 3 2 1

SUNS OF TULANNI

THE BLINDING OF THE SUNS

Chapter One

"The suns are so hot compared to home," Mara covered her eyes and looked skyward. She could feel the burning heat radiating through her boots, even though she had come through the natak only moments before. She watched as the strange doorway closed, seeing Earth for the last time.

As terrible as it would've been to be captured by the Patrol, Mara was already having her doubts about her choice to come to Tuulani. She looked at the never-ending horizon of golden sands. It appeared that they had traded one death sentence for another.

"Let's look for someplace to rest from the heat," Nathan nodded to the others. They looked at him with a shared concern. Mara had just given birth. Now there was no water in sight, nor a cool place for her and the children to hide from the searing heat.

They walked for what seemed hours to Mara, and her exposed skin began to burn. She did not have the protective hair that the Tuulans had, and she stumbled to one knee from the heat and exhaustion. Ket picked her up and cradled her.

"Perhaps a little rest from walking, Mara," Ket stated in a nonchalant manner. He knew how independent his grandson's spouse could be. "You will need to care for your babes soon enough, so take a small rest for yourself." Mara nodded slightly and passed out in Ket's arms. Tan placed a light blanket over her to shade her from the suns. The twin suns they had once dreamt of seeing.

They had travelled four cycles of the suns and the whole entourage was suffering. The days were punishingly hot and the nights were cold. The water rations had dwindled, and the food was almost non-existent. It wouldn't be too long before death found them.

On the fifth day, they found an endless wall of sand that merged with the horizon. They couldn't backtrack. There wasn't any water or food behind them, there was only more sand. Mara thought the obstacle was only a mirage. She had heard of such things happening to those who were desperate for water. The others did not agree with her assessment. Her razor-sharp mind had become more easily confused the past few days. Perhaps it was dehydration and the stress of giving birth. Perhaps.

"What kind of trick could make such an unending reflection?" Tam looked at the others and frowned. "We can't all be sharing the same illusion." His eyes narrowed as he stared at the wall.

Nathan took a deep breath and motioned for the others to move back a little. Without a word, he reached forward and placed his hand halfway into the mirage. When he pulled his hand back, it was covered with sand.

"This is no reflection or mirage," Nathan looked at the twinkling particles shining in the glow of the suns. He looked up at the group. "It is like the waterfalls we had on Earth. Perhaps there is shelter behind it." Nathan had a stern look. "I will be right back."

"Nathan, be careful. We don't…" Mara's words were cut short as she watched her husband disappear beyond the wall. She looked at the Tuulan men and her children.

"If he doesn't come back, I'm going in after him!" Mara finished her idle threat. It made a few men chuckle, even though it was out of nervousness.

Minutes passed and Nathan didn't return. The suns were burning Mara's skin again, and the children were suffering from the relentless heat. The men collected a bit of water from each of their water skins and gave it to Mara and the children. They were the future, and they must not perish.

Minutes turned into hours according to the suns, if they were to be trusted. Mara had no idea of how time actually worked on this world. All she knew was that it seemed an eternity passed each moment she waited.

"He will be back soon, I promise," Mara reassured her children. She hoped, as she promised the unknown, that she was not lying to them.

Nathan held his breath as he walked through the pouring sand. He was slowly drowning, although there was no water. He covered his mouth and nose as he took another shallow breath in the space created by his fingers. He kept moving forward into the unknown.

"All I need to do is find the other side and send back help." Nathan moved his opposite hand to cover his eyes. *"Whether I survive or not, Mara and the children need to find shelter or they will die."* The desperation filled his chest as he pushed harder through the flowing sand.

As quickly as he had entered the flowing wall, the other side finally revealed itself. Nathan spun around and looked at a lush, green oasis that seemed almost too perfect to be real. A short distance from where he stood was a small pond with a large jutting rock next to it.

"Mara," Nathan yelled into the never-ending flow of the sand wall. He heard nothing but the pouring sound of it sinking back into the dune. "Mara," he yelled again in a louder voice, but he knew he wouldn't be getting a response. No one could hear him.

He walked over to the pristine water, took a drink, and sat down. The rocks made an almost perfect seat. He placed his head in his hands as he rested and thought.

He could think of no way to get the others through the wall, and it weighed heavily on his conscience. No matter how hard he concentrated, his mind was completely void of ideas.

Looking up at the beautiful and stark landscape, he realized his home world had a harshness he couldn't overcome. It was a feeling of complete hopelessness he had never encountered before.

Nathan pushed himself back on the rock a bit further to rest his back. It felt as though something shifted, but he ignored the feeling. The heat was playing tricks on his mind.

"You have summoned me," a strange voice echoed behind Nathan. He spun around and saw an odd looking Tuulan floating in mid-air. There was no one else to be found, but she didn't seem real. He could see through her.

"I am Batah. Is there some way I can assist you?"

Nathan cocked his head to one side, trying to determine if this strange conversation was a result of heat exhaustion. Either way, he did not want to be rude. *Rude?* He raised his eyes and looked skyward feeling like an idiot. But, foolish or not, it wouldn't hurt to ask for help.

"My family is on the other side of the wall," he motioned toward the flowing sand. "I need to get them to water or they will die." His eyebrows furrowed as he closed his eyes in desperation. "Can you help me?"

Nathan opened his eyes to determine if he had been delusional, but the visage was still in front of him. He reached out to touch her arm, but his hand passed through. The exchange had not seemed to cause any change in Batah's demeanor.

"That is easily resolved." Batah smiled at Nathan as she gestured toward the rock he had been sitting on. "Just touch the jewel on the top of the marker."

"Marker," Nathan asked as he looked down at the stone and brushed the sand off the top. Under the debris was a shining blue stone. "What does the stone mark?"

"The edge of the City, and the beginning of the Outlands. The blue jewel will open a doorway for your family to pass through, and also show the path to the City," Batah nodded toward the jewel and promptly faded away.

Nathan shook his head and wondered just how crazy the heat had made him. Still… it was an idea. Hallucination or not, Batah's suggestion was a hell of a lot more than he had a few moments ago. He shrugged his shoulders and pushed down on the now twinkling blue circle.

The suns were hot and unforgiving. Mara knew her children and the older Tuulans would soon collapse from the dehydration and heat exhaustion. She didn't even know if Nathan was still alive.

A tear fell as she stared at the place where Nathan had entered the flowing sand. It was hypnotic and deadly, just like the poisoned pools of water on Earth. Death is what they often delivered.

Mara wondered if Nathan had made it to the other side. Or had the sands engulfed him, taking him from her forever. She closed her eyes at the pain of that thought. It was almost too much to bear.

Her eyes snapped open as she remembered the ring Nathan had given her after their bonding. It had bound their hearts together, making it possible for them to feel each other's strongest emotions.

It was glowing as it had done before, and she knew he was still alive. She knew in her heart that he was trying to come back to them. To her.

"Look," Ket yelled. "The sands are parting," he pointed at a small teardrop shaped spot. It was becoming larger by the minute. Mara motioned to the others.

"Quickly…get everyone ready to move. We may not have much time if the sands part enough for us to pass through," Mara looked back at the others. She could see that they were already prepared.

The small opening became larger until it formed an arched door. The sands flowed around it as if it were a solid mass, but there was nothing visible diverting the sands. There, on the other side, stood Nathan looking as incredulous at this turn of events as any of the others.

"Run, Mara! We need to get everyone through. We don't know how long this will last," Nathan yelled through the tunnel of sand. An organized rush pushed through the tunnel. Every single soul made it to the other side.

A flash came from the blue circle. The sands slowly closed and the arched tunnel completely disappeared. With that completed, the unending dunes behind Nathan disappeared, revealing a city a short distance away.

No one could speak. So much had happened in the last few days, there were no words that were adequate. The small group rested a short while at the oasis before they walked the last portion of their journey.

BLOOD AND TEARS

Chapter Two

"**M**other?!" A young voice was yelling at Mara and was apparently irritated that she had not responded. Mara had been thinking of their arrival on Tuulani and the events that had occurred since that day. It had been a traumatic journey from the first moment her boots stepped onto the sands.

"Yes Tammy? What is it?" Mara asked, shaking the daydream out of her head.

"Finally!" Tamara answered, exasperated. She took a deep breath to calm herself. "You need to come down to the hall. Tasira is crying. This time they threw something at her."

Mara quickly ran down the stairs to the main hall. There in the corner was her little Tasira, gasping for breath as she continued to cry. Her face was red and there was a long scratch down her arm.

"Tasira," Mara said softly. The young girl ran so quickly to her mother she almost fell along the way. Mara stroked the little one's hair and steered her towards her bedroom.

"They ha...hate me," Tasira hiccupped as she spoke. "Why do they hate me Mama? I've never been mean to them. Why can't they just leave me alone? "

"I don't know Tasira, but this is the last time you will need to go to school with them. I will talk to U'na and ask if she can give you your lessons in a different way. We will work on them together, alright?" Mara said softly, brushing the tears from her little one's eyes. She helped her up and gave her to Ket. He nodded and brought Tasira up the stairs toward her bedroom.

A loud banging on the door startled Mara for a second. The door opened and smacked against the wall before Mara could open it. In a dramatic, arrogant flourish D'kal and her son Foro came into the foyer. Foro was sporting the beginnings of a black eye and a few other minor scrapes. D'kal stomped toward Tamara pointing her finger at the child.

"You...you little half-breed. If you ever touch my son again, I'll make sure you never see another day." D'kal sneered at Tamara in disdain.

"You shouldn't have even been born. In the old days, you would have been thrown outside the wall, into the Outlands, like any other unwanted trash. You are an aberration of the natural order..." D'kal continued to rage at Tammy. The young Tuulan stood her ground, folded her arms and narrowed her eyes. She didn't have to say a word. D'kal took further insult and raised her hand to strike Tamara. Mara's hand clenched around the Kuutaran's wrist, staring at her while she made her point.

"You touch my child and *we* will have a problem. Do you understand me?" Mara's tone was flat and threatening. D'kal smiled at Mara with an air of superiority as she yanked her hand back from Mara's tight grasp.

"You do not have the ability, or right, to challenge me," she stated, looking Mara up and down. "Human!" she spat out.

"My home is the moon that circles Tuulani. The Tuulans and Kuutaran's have a long history and shared ancestry. We and the Tuulans are the only ones with true blood and the right of ascension. We are the ones destined to be rulers, not some Human *haasa* that wound up here by mistake." D'kal smiled and tossed her dark blue hair back. Mara smiled blandly back at D'kal.

"It is strange that the chosen race has had no female children, isn't it? Perhaps I am not the one who is trash after all. Good day, D'kal." Mara finished and held out her hand to Tamara, dismissing the woman as if she was no longer worthy of discussion. Mara and Tammy turned to walk away, hand in hand. Tamara smiled at her mother, knowing that her mother was protecting her as she had protected Tasira.

Like Mara, it was the young woman's nature to be protective. She had studied her mother diligently as Mara practiced her self-defense exercises. The Patrol on Earth had provided the training Mara had needed, but now it was Tamara who had proven herself adept during the training exercises. Mara's oldest daughter was growing larger and stronger every day and soon she would have the ability to handle herself in any situation.

Suddenly, Tamara felt her mother's hand squeeze hers. She had sensed that the issue with D'kal was not finished. Tammy looked up at Mara and saw the slightest nod of her mother's head.

"This conversation has not ended, *Human*." D'kal screamed at Mara. Mara stopped, not turning around as she spoke.

"You are mistaken D'kal. I have nothing further to say to you." The room was quiet for a moment. "You may leave now," Mara finished in an even tone. The outraged cry came as soon as Mara finished speaking. The heavy sound of footsteps came closer until Mara could wait no longer.

"Now, Tammy!" she yelled as the two separated and took a battle stance.

D'kal's large frame came at Mara and Foro turned his attention toward Tamara. D'kal took a swing at Mara with her black, razor sharp nails, barely missing Mara's face. Mara twirled around elegantly and reached her practice staff, still standing against the wall. She again twirled back to D'kal's side and swung the staff hard into the Kuutaran's midsection, taking the breath from her larger opponent. D'kal bent over and gasped for air.

Foro did not have the swiftness of his mother. He, instead, ran towards Tamara using his head as a battering ram. It was not the best idea that the young man could have devised. Tammy, seeing that Foro was coming at her in such a manner, backed up and then sidestepped Foro. His head hit the wall behind Tammy, knocking him out cold.

"What goes on here?" yelled Ket, seeing the "guests" he had just heard entering their home were lying on the floor.

"Grandfather, they attacked us!" Tamara looked to her mother who nodded at the girl to continue. "Mother and I were walking away from them and they tried to take the advantage of our backs turned." She looked down where D'kal lay.

"They have no honor!" Tamara finished with an angry clip to her voice. She was breathing heavily with indignation. Ket cocked his head to one side and looked at Tamara intently.

"Their honor, or lack of it, is not your judgment to make. Run now and get your father. We will need help bringing these two back to their home."

"I need no help from this family," D'kal breathed heavily as she got up. "Not a single one of you will be touching my child again. I will see us home safely." D'kal walked slowly toward her son and gathered him up in her arms. Her eyes narrowed as she walked past Mara and spat on the floor.

"We will finish this another time, *du'lupa*." Ket placed his large hand on Mara's shoulder as the Kuutaran walked past her, opening the door and slamming it shut.

"What did D'kal call you mother?" Tamara asked with a furrowed brow.

"It makes no difference, Tammy." Mara stated quietly as she looked at Ket. "It is a bad thing to call anyone, and that is all you need to know. And, young lady, I had better not hear it coming from your lips!"

"Well, how do I know it is bad if I do not know what it means?" Tamara asked, raising one eyebrow as she looked at her great-grandfather and her mother. Ket rolled his eyes towards the sky, shaking his head.

"You are definitely your mother's daughter!" he stated, exasperated. "I will tell you what it means if you promise to never use the word...in any language," he finished, shaking a finger at the young girl. Tamara nodded, her eyes shining with anticipation at learning something so forbidden.

"The Kuutaran word 'du'lupa', is the same as the Human word 'whore'. Do you know what that means?" Ket asked Tamara. The young girl shook her head, she had never heard such a word before. Ket sighed.

"It means a female who does not have one mate, but has relations with many males for a reward of some kind. Do you understand, now, why your mother does not want you to say such a word to anyone?" he paused a moment, looking at her embarrassed face.

"Sometimes it is better not to know such things, do you not agree, little one?" Ket finished with a stern look on his face. Tamara gave Ket and Mara a nod, barely being able to look them in the eyes.

"I will be in my room if you need me," Tamara stated in a quiet voice. She started up the stairs and abruptly stopped. She turned around and ran back to Mara.

"I am sorry mother," she said as flung her arms around Mara. "I promise I will try to be better. If I hadn't hit Foro, none of this would have happened," she finished; a tear tumbled down her face onto Mara's shoulder.

"I am glad that you stood up for your sister, Tammy. Maybe next time, though, we can find another way besides violence? It is best to use your skill only when it is a matter of life or death." Mara hugged her daughter and pointed her towards the stairs. "Go practice your studies now, we can talk more later." Ket and Mara watched Tamara disappear into the upper hallway.

"You know this is only the start Mara. D'kal's family will not let this rest. I will find Nathan and tell him of this...incident," Ket stated solemnly. Mara nodded at the old Tuulan. This was all they needed when so much was already happening.

Chapter Three

Ket went to the House of the Elders which lay in the center of town. By the whispered comments and unsettled feeling in the city, it was apparent that D'kal's voice had spread her version of events already. Ket was sure she had played the part of a devoted mother and that her son was the injured party. This was not the way Nathan would win the hearts of the city residents, and the right of ascension.

Ket shuddered to think what would happen if D'kal's house won the right. To be more precise, it was the house of Tavon.

But the real power would be D'kal. She had married the old Tuulan only for the power it gave her. Tavon was too easily persuaded by drink and females to ever be the *Ra Shan* of the city. The Ra Shan needed to have both strength and compassion, and Tavon had neither.

Tavon would show the qualities that D'kal wanted him to show, and that would be the end of any peaceful existence. Even the naming of the town would be determined by the Ra Shan. It was yet another power D'kal wished to have.

The selection of a Ra Shan was ancient and steeping in tradition. But it was still a poor substitute for the original right of succession, the Commencement of the Priestess. In centuries past, a young woman was chosen by Tuulani itself to protect and rule over the planet. The old stories told that the suns and wind themselves would bow to the priestess, and she would have domain over everything the planet held and beyond.

Ket was so deep in thought that it seemed that only a few minutes had passed when he reached the House of the Elders. He was not looking forward to telling Nathan about the fight that had ensued after his little Tasira had been injured. Ket walked with a dread that slowed his pace considerably as he reached the main hall and his grandson, Nathan.

Mara was in the house, reading to her children. There had been so much information in the box her grandfather had left for her that it had taken a while to get through it all. She savored every word from her own world, and took every opportunity to reread the documents to her children.

On Earth, Grandfather had said that the stories he told her were only the beginning and that she should study, in secret, the information she would find. He could have never imagined that Mara would have the freedom to study the papers and books whenever she wished. He was only thinking of her living on Earth where the Council controlled everything. Where unapproved education and possession of the knowledge in the box could mean execution.

Mara stopped for a second to look up at her fidgety group of children. Nathaniel and Tamara were trying to keep the younger two in line and Tasira was staring blankly into the floor. She smiled. She knew they were trying their best.

"Should we go see what Caleb has found for you five to eat?" Mara asked brightly. Four went on ahead to the kitchen, but Mara remained behind with Tasira. It was obvious that she was completely miserable. Her smallest child was always the most sensitive of her five children and had been having a hard time adjusting to life on Tuulani.

"What would you like to do, Tasira?" Mara asked. Tasira continued looking at the floor as she shrugged her shoulders. Mara grabbed her little one's hands.

"Let's go find an adventure together. We'll need some supplies though. Shall we go and have a quick snack with the others and then go off somewhere together?" Tasira looked up at her mother and nodded with excitement. She continued to hold her mother's hand as they walked toward the kitchen.

Two hours later the two adventure seekers were walking through the oldest part of the house. There was a quietness about this part of the house that seemed to salve Tasira's wounds. The old architecture revealed hidden archways and staircases and made Tasira's sadness melt away into laughter. They spent hours in the old wing of the house until the suns started to tumble into the horizon.

"We had best go back now or the others will think we are lost!" Mara told her daughter. Tasira nodded.

"Can I come back here tomorrow? Please Mama?" The young girl's eyes pleaded with her mother. Mara looked around. There was nothing in the structure that could harm her. She and Tasira had already looked in every room. It was safe and would keep Tasira occupied. She had the normal curiosity of a girl of twelve years even though she was much younger in Human years. It was the nature of the Tuulans to mature at a much faster rate, and then conversely, live longer. Tasira, though, had not matured as quickly as Tamara had, emotionally.

"If you promise to keep up with your studies, you can come here anytime you want to get away. O.K?" Mara stated.

"I promise." Tasira said seriously. And with that decided, they went back to the main house to find the others.

Chapter Four

Nathan sighed as he reached his home. The meeting with the Elders had not gone well from the beginning, and the appearance of an outraged D'kal and her whining son was a sickening show to watch. The Elders had already decided that further deliberation would be needed to decide the proper course of action.

The Right of Ascension was a serious matter and could not be left to a common vote; there must be secondary validation of the decision. The debate had lasted for hours until D'kal arrived. Afterwards, the meeting was halted and the Elders told Nathan to go to his home and find out the truth from his family's perspective. He was instructed to return in the morning, with Mara and Tamara, to tell their side of the issue.

As he walked through the doorway to the meeting hall, a clamor of bare feet could be heard running towards him. The children must have been watching for their father to return. An uproar of five young voices sounded at the same time making their case for their mother.

"Alright! Alright! All of you quiet down right now! I know that you all want to tell me what happened, but I can't understand what you're saying if you all speak at once!" Nathan stated in a loud, rumbling voice. The uproar stopped immediately and the children looked up at their father with wide eyes; he had never spoken to them in such a tone.

"Now...one by one, you can come into my study and tell me your version of what happened today. You can only tell me what you actually saw and heard, yourself, and nothing more. Do you understand?" Nathan finished on a gentler note. All five faces looked up at him and nodded almost simultaneously.

"Good. I will start with Tamara." He stated as he ushered his oldest female child into his study. Each child went into their father's study and told him exactly what they had seen and heard. Nathan wrote it down on the Hermes paper he had gently harvested from the sacred tree on his way into his house.

Hermes paper was the only paper allowed into the official record of the Elders. Nathan was very careful how he wrote the information. Errors could only be crossed out, and the paper could not be discarded. Even scraps and trimmings were brought to the Hall of Elders to give nourishment to the soil of the tree that covered the Hall from the suns. It was sacred and there were consequences for not treating it as such.

The next day, Nathan, Mara and Tasira walked to the Hall of the Elders with the document carefully placed inside a folder. This document and Mara and Tasira's testimony were the only two things that could save Nathan's house from being removed from the Elder's list. If that were to happen, D'kal's family would have no obstacles in their way. Tavon would ascend as Ra Shan of the city.

Jes was an ancient Tuulan, born on the home world and was now the Head Elder. He would make all announcements regarding the Ascension and all matters brought to the Hall. The remaining eight Elders often did not speak at all.

The change from the Hall of Elders rule and the reign of a Ra Shan was arduous for the elders and not all of them were sure it was a valid choice for the city. But today, there was a more immediate concern being presented. D'kal's charge that members of the House of Nathan attacked her and her son without provocation.

Violence, of any type, was a serious matter. Jes motioned to Nathan and Tavon to come forward and present their record of events. Nathan nodded.

"Here is the record from my family, written on the sacred paper. The scraps are held in a wool bag my wife made," stated Nathan as he handed over the box that held both items. Tavon walked up to the Elders with a swagger in his step.

"Here is my family's statement regarding Nathan's daughters' and wife's unprovoked attack on my wife and little boy. The scraps from the paper are held in the finest hekhalot cloth. To do less is a travesty," finished Tavon. He turned his head toward Nathan, face without emotion but an evil twinkle in his eye.

"We have received the statements and, once read, they will be added to the official record of the Elders. Now go home and wait while we contemplate this issue. We will call on each of you when it is time to render the decision." With that stated, the entire group of Elders rose from their seats and turned their backs on the two men as they walked away.

Chapter Five

The weeks following the incident brought new challenges to Nathan and Mara. The city had been divided in their allegiances and the tension in the city and in Nathan's home had grown each passing week. Nathan and Mara did their best to keep their extended family happy and safe, but after the last week, Tamara was sent home from school for her own safety.

The two girls had their own ways to play to keep their minds challenged. Tamara practiced self-defense every morning with her mother and studied the fighting methods of any race or species she could find in the books of the library.

Tasira, however, barely finished her studies at all. She was often in the oldest wing of the house, imagining everything from being a princess to an archeological scientist. Her vivid imagination spun her into a happy cocoon that made her feel safe.

"Mama?" Tasira yelled for Mara.

"Yes, Tasira. What is it you need?" Came Mara's voice from the other room.

"Can I take a lunch and spend the day in the old castle?"

Mara fought the smile as she walked into the other room. "So, it is a castle now, is it?" She went over to her daughter and gave her a hug.

"Oh yes, Mama! With a princess and jewels and so many rooms that I can't count them all!" She replied breathlessly.

"That princess wouldn't happen to have the name Tasira, would she?" Mara asked with a smile.

Tasira blushed a little. "Maybe," she stated shyly. "But can I go, Mama? Please?" She asked pleadingly, her big green eyes looking up at her mother.

"Alright, Your Highness. Pack a lunch and be on your way. Just remember to be back before the suns go below the horizon, O.K.?"

"I promise." She said solemnly and quickly ran off in the direction of the kitchen.

Mara chuckled as she watched her daughter run off to her newest adventure. If only real life could be chased away with such happiness. What a wonderful place that would be to live.

Nathan was in his study, trying to figure out the best way to run the new water system for the city. He had already come up with a plan for planting and harvesting the crops. He also found that the best way to store the commodities was to utilize the old ways of drying them in the sun. Foods could also be sealed in large vases with sap from the mahdo plant. When heated, mahdo rendered into a substance much like the putty made from the hooves of the ezza'a, reminiscent of the sheep of Earth.

The only difference between the ezza'a putty and the mahdo sap, was when it cooled. Mahdo rendered sap was very hard and had no taste or odor. He knew the younger ones were going to laugh at the idea, but sometimes it is best to respect the old ways. The Ancestors survived and thrived by respecting nature. Returning to the simple ways could work. He was deep in these thoughts when he sensed he had a visitor.

"Hello Father," stated Nathaniel, "May I speak with you?" he finished in a serious, adult tone. Nathan stared at the young man and nodded.

"What is it that you need to tell me Nathaniel? I have a great amount of work to complete before the

Elders call for me, and I have run into some difficulties." He looked up at his son.

Nathaniel cleared his throat as if he were planning to make a speech to an assembly. It made Nathan smile a little bit as he turned his head away from the child.

"I know that this incident with Mother, Tammy and Tasira has caused you problems Father. I want you to tell the Elders that it was my fault. Let them punish me however they want to, I do not care." Nathaniel went to his father and laid his hand on Nathan's large arm.

"I do not want them to succeed. It would be very bad for everyone if Tavon became Ra Shan. The whole city would suffer. It would become the same as it was on Earth." Nathaniel finished, his eyes pleading with his father. Nathan pulled up a chair for his son and motioned for him to sit down.

"Nathaniel," Nathan started, his eyes shining with pride at his son's self-sacrificing words.

"I am proud that you would do this for us, for the city, but it would not be the right thing to do. You did not have anything to do with the fight that day. You cannot build anything of value on a lie. We will manage this together as a family. Whatever the decision the Elders make, I know that we have all done our best and have acted honorably." Nathaniel looked at the floor and then back up at his father. Nathan grabbed his son's arms gently, "Now I must continue with my thoughts on the best way to improve the city," Nathan stated as he returned to his desk.

"May I stay with you?" Nathaniel asked. Nathan looked at the young man and nodded.

"Perhaps you will have other ideas that we can explore together." Nathaniel nodded his head and smiled. It was the first time Nathan had seen his son smile for a very long time.

Tasira was enjoying the life of a princess in her imaginary castle, but the game became boring after the first hour. She packed up her blanket "robe", and other princess trappings, and decided it was time to change the game. She was going to be an archeologist. She was sure she would find a lost treasure that would be capable of changing bullies to rodents.

That's it, she would transform Foro into a rat that would be chased around the town. Tasira nodded and started looking around even though she and her mother had been in every room in the wing.

Tasira had played for a couple of hours before she realized she was hungry. She stopped in the over-sized room and placed her blanket on the floor. She carefully set out the food she had brought along and realized she had more food than she could eat. She looked at the fruit, the cheese sandwich, the biscuits, and the vegetable that Caleb made her pack. She made a face at that, not really liking any of the roots and leaves Caleb made her eat. *"It will make you big and strong like your sister,"* she heard his voice in her head. Tasira sighed at the thought. She was never going to be as big as Tammy and she knew it. The other children often took advantage of her small stature and she knew she was the reason that her father's bid for Ra Shan was at risk.

Tasira picked up the sandwich and decided she would eat half now and half later. As she tore the flat bread and cheese into two pieces, she saw a glint of light on the opposite wall from where she placed her picnic. She saw it for a split second again and then another beam of light that lasted long enough for her to make a shadow in the light with her hand. She looked behind her and saw the last blip of light disappear from her view. It came from one of the stones where the wall and floor met.

She took out the piece of charcoal Caleb had given her to use in her drawings. She wanted to mark the stone so she could find it again after she went home when the suns fell down on the horizon. As she went to mark the stone, she stumbled and her hand fell upon it. The whole room glowed with the strange light and a portion of the wall disappeared completely showing a staircase that went down into total darkness. Tasira stepped into the doorway and lights appeared on the staircase. She followed them a bit further and as she went, more lights showed illuminated the way.

The lights were beautiful and entrancing. Until she turned around and saw that the door had closed behind her.

"No!" she screamed. "Let me out!" She ran to the top of the staircase. As before, the opening appeared and she could walk out into the room she had just left. Tasira's heart was beating so hard she could not breathe steadily. She scooped up her things and ran back to the safety of the home she knew and her mother's arms.

Chapter Six

"Telora! Get out of the kitchen!" Mara stated to her youngest in exasperation. "Caleb and I cannot cook if you keep taking our ingredients!" She looked at the young girl who had berry juice and flour all over her shirt. She tried not to smile, but Telora looked at her with big green eyes and Mara started to laugh. Telora and Caleb soon joined in, making the scolding voice completely ineffective.

"All right, you two, that will be enough," she finished with as much of the stern face she could again muster.

"These young females definitely take after their mother," Caleb smiled. "They have a mind of their own and will use their charm to win over anyone they can," he finished, chuckling. "I think you have your work set for you, Mara." The old Tuulan shook his head and walked to the pantry to get additional berries. As he walked, he whistled for Mara to look his way. He motioned to the other side of the kitchen where Telora's twin, Ketasha was sitting in a corner with berries mashed in her hand, causing a steady drip of purple juice from her hand.

"Ketasha!" Mara yelled. "Get over here and let's get you both cleaned up," she stated, swooping both girls up to the bathtub which still needed to be filled. Mara met Tam on her way, "Can you help me get the water ready for these two?" she asked in a stressed voice.

Tam raised his eyebrows, but nodded yes. *"She can fight like a warrior, but those two little ones can distract her? May the Priestess help anyone who tries to actually harm her family,"* he thought as he rolled his eyes upward. He went to get the water ready while Mara peeled off the girls' shirts and dresses.

Mara was stripping the little girls and readying them for a bath upstairs when Tasira came into the kitchen. "Uncle Caleb, where is Mother?" Tasira said in a ragged breath. Caleb noticed all of her princess clothing and food was haphazardly thrown together. Caleb looked at Tasira with solemn face.

"I would put all of my things where they belong if I were a princess who was a little late in coming back," he finished, raising his eyebrows to convey the seriousness of his words. "Your mother is with the twins and they have made quite a mess for her to clean up. I would wait for the right time to talk to her," he said, helping her put her food away, "and this is not the right time, trust me." he stated. Tasira nodded and walked into her room to put her playthings away. She would just have to tell Mother later.

With the evening meal finally prepared and served, all in the House of Nathan sat at the large table to eat. The talk was sporadic until Tasira piped into the adult's lack of conversation.

"I went to the castle today and I found a glowing staircase," Tasira said in excitement. "I didn't go all of the way down the stairs because I was scared of not being able to come back!"

"Tasira! Mother and Father do not need to hear your fairy tales tonight, they have important things on their minds," Nathaniel stated, trying to sound grown up. Nathan's mouth twitched a little at his son's attempt to sound in charge.

"But it is *not* a fairy tale, Nathaniel!" She looked at him with her brow furrowed and her bottom lip pouting just a bit. "I *did* see a glowing staircase!" Mara looked at her son and sighed. Nathaniel knew he had overstepped his authority, and now looked at his plate as if the food was the most interesting thing he had ever seen.

Mara looked over at Tasira. "So where was this staircase?"

"In one of the big rooms we were in looking for treasures." Tasira answered, relieved that Nathaniel hadn't spoiled her story. "I sat down to have part of my sandwich and the staircase appeared right behind me. Mara nodded, trying to look enthusiastic in spite of her exhaustion.

"Well, I am quite sure that if the staircase appeared to you, it must be meant for only you. Don't you think?" she asked, looking around the table for support.

"Oh, yes Tasira!" Caleb chimed in, "It must be your very own special staircase. You are the Princess, are you not?" With that said, all of the other men jumped in to let Tasira know that what her mother had said must be true.

"Perhaps you should visit it again tomorrow!" Tasira's grandfather Ket said to her with a wink of his eye. "You aren't afraid of the staircase, are you? I mean, if you are too scared to go back, I would understand." Ket stated. His tone of voice was both supportive and goading. The young girl had to face some of her fears and the best place to start would be her own home. Tasira narrowed her eyes and looked at all of the faces at the table.

"I am not scared. I just wanted to let you know what I found." Tasira straightened her spine a little, "I will go back tomorrow," she stated with a nod. The men all smiled to themselves, thinking they had helped to quell the little one's fears.

The morning suns were shining brightly on the covers in Nathan and Mara's bedroom. Mara turned over and kissed the over-sized shoulder of her mate. Nathan smiled with his eyes still closed.

"Too bad Nathan is so tired," Mara whispered across Nathan's chest as her hand played softly with his hair. "I will go and practice my morning defense exercises so that my mate can sleep," she finished smirking. Nathan swiftly flipped Mara on her back, his face directly over hers.

"Perhaps not right now," he smiled. Mara laughed as their play became more amorous. She kissed Nathan deeply and looked into his eyes. The smile that had been there before was replaced with a passion that engulfed both Mara and Nathan.

Mara had not used the woman's medallion since she had left Earth. When she presented it to the Hall of Elders, they had decided that Mara should have the right to keep the medallion to herself if she wished. But Mara knew that it would be wrong to keep it to herself. There would have to be more female children born if the Tuulans were to survive and the medallion was the key to solving that problem. The weight of that burden played heavily on Mara's mind.

She knew that the ship that had carried the few female Tuulans back to Tuulani had never arrived. The remaining medallions were now lost on other planets, and with them the hope of having other female children. All of the residents of the city bore only male offspring just as it had been for many generations. No other women, brought back to Tuulani, were capable of having female children. Only Mara.

It was if the twin suns themselves were conspiring. They were judging and punishing the Tuulans for the mistakes made by their ancestors. Now, it seemed, the choice of changing that fate was up to her. But where to begin.

It was an hour later when Mara and Nathan made their appearance for the morning meal. A few of the men still remained at the table and smiled knowingly at the two. Mara had long since lost her embarrassment with the openness of the talk between the members of

Nathan's home and smiled back. A very excited Tasira ran up to her parents.

"May I go to the staircase again today?" Both Tamara and Nathaniel rolled their eyes at their sister's excitement.

"You should be doing something to help Mother and Father instead of running after daydreams," Tamara told her sister with note of disapproval in her voice. "There are real problems at our home and you should help solve them instead of running away." Tammy paused for a moment. "I will be finishing my studies and then I will train the rest of the day with my defense exercises." Nathaniel joined in.

"I will finish my studies. Then I will help Father. What have you done to help, Tasira?" He looked at his small sister haughtily.

Mara saw the twinge of Tasira's chin before the young girl lowered her eyes. She then looked at the two older children. She pointed at each of them when she spoke.

"You, Tamara," she said pointedly, "And you, young man, are not the adults of this house. You have no right to speak to anyone in the tone of voice I just heard you use. I know your intent is to help your father and me, but you have no right to determine what is and is not helpful when it comes to other family members." Mara looked at Tammy and the Nathaniel sternly, "Now you will apologize to Tasira for making her sad." Nathaniel looked at his sister reluctantly, not wanting to apologize at all. But his mother's pointing finger was something he was not willing to test.

"I am sorry Tasira," he said rather stiffly. Mara then pointed at Tamara. The girl squirmed a little under the pressure to do the right thing.

"I am sorry too, Tasira," she stated petulantly with a slight flush to her face.

"Now, since you two are done with your meal, you will go to your rooms and complete those studies you spoke of so proudly. After you are finished, you can come downstairs and help Caleb in the kitchen." That statement got some grumbling that was quickly quelled with just a look from their father. Mara continued.

"And when that is done and Caleb says you may leave, then you may go to help your father or practice your defense training." She looked her two pouting children and nodded. That was the only encouragement they needed to remove themselves from the disapproving looks of the adults at the table. Mara turned to Tasira.

"Now, little one. Go and get your things packed and we will go on an adventure today. We will see where this staircase goes and what treasures it reveals Princess." Tasira smiled brightly and nodded as she grabbed flatbread to make sandwiches, cheese, dried fruit and went to the kitchen to fill two water skins for their adventure. With the children fed, Mara and Nathan started to fill their plates with food.

They had just begun, when they heard the loud banging at the front door. Nathan turned around and saw that Tam was running towards them. In his hand he held a piece of paper.

"We have problems outside," Tam stated in an ominous tone. "Take a look at what D'kal and her mate Tavon have done." He placed the paper in Mara's hand. Mara opened the now crumpled paper and was sickened by what she read.

"The Earth female, Mara, has been keeping a terrible secret. She has a woman's medallion from a Tuulan female who died at the hands of her people. She took the medallion from the dead female and used it to ensure that she alone would have female children. Mara, from the House of Nathan, must pay for her crimes against the Tuulan race. We will be petitioning the Hall of Elders for the medallion and a suitable punishment for the Human female."

For Tuulani,

The House of Tavon for the Tuulan race."

"They want the medallion, Nathan," Mara closed her eyes and leaned back in her chair. "They want the medallion and my blood on their hands." She opened her eyes and looked at her husband. She was weary of the constant fight for the Right of Ascension, weary of the attacks on her family.

"The Elders told you it was yours to do with as you deemed correct." The anger shone in Nathan's eyes. "This is some insane plan to ensure Tavon is chosen for the Ra Shan, and nothing more. I will go the House of the Elders and settle this matter now!" Nathan started to rise from his seat to leave as Mara placed a hand on his arm.

"It will not matter, Nathan. The path has been set for us." Mara looked around at Ket, Pel, Tam and the others at the table. "This matter is now beyond the realm of the Elders. Tavon and D'kal have begun to rally the city against us. This is just the beginning." Mara rose from her chair and walked slowly towards her bedroom.

Tasira watched quietly from the kitchen doorway. She had never felt so scared in her short life. She knew what she had to do. She would find the treasure the staircase led to. That would protect her mother. Tasira quietly gathered her packed items and ran off toward the old wing of the house.

Chapter Seven

The mass of people outside the House of Nathan had been getting larger. Tuulans, old and young, began yelling obscenities about Mara and throwing stones at Nathan as he went outside. This went on for days, and then a week. On the tenth day, Nathan would take no more. Nathan stepped outside of his door to answer a knock, a rock hit him in the chest.

"Get out of here!" He roared. The crowd stopped and a silent awe quieted even the most fervent of the Tuulan mob. They had never heard such a rage before and many of them left quietly and never returned. When they left, a small Kuutaran female was standing in front of Nathan.

"If you are here on D'kal's request, you can leave now!" he yelled at the young girl. She took a step back, but did not leave.

"No, Father," Nathan heard his son call out, "she is here because of me." The young Nathaniel looked at his father pleadingly.

"Are you insane?" Nathan asked incredulously. "It is her mother who began this chaos and it is her mother who wants *your* mother's blood on her hands!" Nathan was breathing heavily now, incensed at this turn of events.

"Qata is not her mother." Nathaniel looked at his father in defiance. "She has done nothing to deserve your anger. She and I have been...friends...for many months now, and I asked her to come to see me at my home. She is here at my request, Father."

Nathan looked at his son and it wasn't too difficult to see that he was in love with the girl. When Qata looked at Nathan in apprehension, he could also see she was not their enemy. He put his large hand on her shoulder and smiled.

"I am sorry, Qata. Please come in to our home." If living with Mara had taught him anything, it was that accepting others despite their differences is the only way to stop hatred. Mara had accepted him unconditionally when no one else, not even his own kind, would. Qata looked at Nathan briefly as she walked into the safety of the foyer.

"Thank you," she said with a shy smile. "Although I am from D'kal's house, I am not her daughter. I was abandoned by my real father when my own mother died of a sickness." Qata shrugged her shoulders, "I guess I looked too much like my mother. He couldn't bear the pain of seeing me every day, so he brought me to D'kal's village on Kuutarii." Nathan motioned for the young girl to sit down on a chair in the Great Hall of his home. Qata sat down and continued.

"D'kal took me in as a way for her to marry Tavon. She told me to pretend that I was her own daughter. It was the only way she could convince Tavon that she was capable of conceiving a daughter." She looked again at Nathaniel and smiled.

"Nathaniel and I have been seeing each other in secret. We didn't know if either family would accept us. He told his mother about me before the first...uh...incident happened. She did not tell you?" Qata asked.

"No, she didn't tell me anything about you. She has been under too much stress lately. I'm sure it did not enter her mind," Nathan commented. "Or maybe she didn't tell me for another reason." He paused for a moment and then sent Jonathan to Mara's room. It wasn't too long before Mara appeared in the doorway of the Great Hall, where the entire house gathered for meals. Now, however, the whole house was gathering to hear the story of Nathaniel and Qata.

"Qata, you are taking a risk coming to our home," Mara told the young girl. "Do you not understand what this could mean if D'kal hears of this? She will use you to get what she wants and then you will disappear like the servants who disobey her. You must leave quickly before she finds you here." Mara finished in a rush of words.

"She does not care. She has thrown me out of her house forever. She knows that Nathaniel and I love one another. She told me that I betrayed her and that she never wanted to see me again." Qata finished as a tear raced down her face.

"Please don't send me away! I will be your servant if you wish." Tears were now coming steadily. "If I cannot stay here, she will have me killed and no one will miss me. Please let me stay with your family." The girl looked pleadingly at Mara and then Nathan. Nathan walked to the other side of the room and motioned to Mara to join him.

"Did you forget this little tidbit of information, or did you think I was such a fool that I would never find out?" He whispered in anger. "What were you thinking? Do you know the dilemma your little secret has caused?"

He whispered loudly. Mara grabbed his arm, pulled him into the kitchen and shut the door.

"Did it ever occur to you that I wanted to protect you from this 'little tidbit' as you call it?" Mara asked angrily. "When I found out about Qata, she and our son were not involved with one another. It was after the fight with D'kal that Nathaniel spoke to Qata and she told him the truth about her family. They had never spoken before that day." Mara's voice got a little louder.

"In fact, I did not know about their relationship until last evening. By the time you came home from the Hall of Elders, it was late. There was no time to tell you until now," Mara said defensively. Nathan smirked and then started to laugh. Mara looked at him as if he had lost his mind.

"We cannot deny Nathaniel's lineage. We certainly caused our share of grief to the men in the village on your home world," he finished, his eyes twinkling. "I think it would be a travesty if we were to keep those two apart. Don't you agree?" Mara smiled back at her husband.

"I think Qata would be a nice addition to the House of Nathan." With that settled, they went out to the Great Hall, hand-in-hand, to tell the others.

When D'kal found out about Qata's new home, she and Tavon went to the Hall of Elders with a formal charge of holding Qata against her will.

"She is but a child and does not understand the treachery of Mara and her half-breed children." Tavon pleaded in a well-rehearsed voice. "That *haasa* will do nothing but poison our little girl's mind," he continued.

"I beg you to force the return of our daughter to us. This awful crime has taken its toll on my wife D'kal." Tavon motioned to the grief-stricken Kuutaran sitting on a bench in the corner, sobbing uncontrollably. "This act, in itself, should show you the true nature of Nathan and his wife. May the Priestess save us from having to serve under Nathan as the Ra Shan!" He finished in a flourish of emotional drama. Jes, the oldest in the Hall of Elders, stood up slowly to speak for the others.

"Because of the seriousness of this charge, we will need to speak to Nathan and his wife as well. We will inform you of our judgment after we have been presented with all of the facts. You may leave for now, but we will send for you when the House of Nathan has been notified and appears in the chamber." And with that, the Elders stood and walked single file until they disappeared behind the large doors at the end of the hall. As Tavon and D'kal left they looked at one another and smiled slightly.

They had what they wanted. They couldn't care less what happened to that little brat Qata.

Chapter Eight

For weeks, Tasira had visited the old wing of her home frequently. It took a couple of days for her to gather the courage to actually walk all the way down the staircase. But what she found was worth the wait. Nestled in the heavy layers of dust were little clear jewels of many colors and books of drawings. The jewels were pretty, but Tasira couldn't figure out what they were for, if anything at all. She gathered them all together in an old dish of some kind. She had been searching every day, but the only thing she ever found was more dust.

Tasira walked past an odd painting on the wall with her princess jewels. As she walked by, the jewels lit up and a voice spoke to her.

"Hello, my name is Batah. How may I assist you?" the voice asked. Tasira wasn't sure if she should run or ask the voice a question. She took a deep breath, and decided to be brave.

"Where are you? I cannot see you, Batah."

"I am very sorry. Perhaps if you brush off the artifact behind you, you will be able to see me. It has been many years since I have functioned in this room."

"Artifact? What artifact?" Tasira spun around and looked. "Do you mean the painting on the wall?" she asked of the disembodied voice.

"Yes. I suppose you could call it a painting. Brush it off until you see a piece of stone that is square and is not even with the other stones." Batah replied.

Tasira did as Batah requested and was surprised to discover just how much dust was covering the wall. The odd painting was actually dust layered over an indented panel. The square stone was easy to find after the dust was gone.

"Batah, I have found the stone. What do I do next?" she asked looking all around her for the woman who had spoken to her.

"Good work, little one! Now press the square stone down until it is even with the others," the voice instructed her.

Tasira completed the task and before her appeared a beautiful Tuulan woman. She wasn't real though, Tasira decided. She could see right through her.

"What are you Batah? I have never seen a person like you before," Tasira asked her in naive innocence.

"That is because I am not a real person. I am just what remains of the real Batah who created me more than a millennia ago. I have not been activated in this room for over seven hundred years. I did talk to a male Tuulan at the edge of the Outlands. That was more than two Earth years ago. He was worried about his family on the other side of the security barrier. He had pushed through the barrier by sheer will. No one had ever survived that journey before. It was the place your mother called the Waterfall of Sand."

"That was my father!" Tasira exclaimed excitedly. "He thought he had just imagined you!" Tasira was so excited that she was bouncing on her toes. The movement caused the pretty jewels to light up again.

"I see you have found all of the books. There is much information to be gained by reading what our ancestors had to say." Batah paused for a minute and looked at the girl quizzically. "May I ask your name, little one?" she asked. Tasira looked at the visage and apologized.

"I am very sorry. I was so excited that I forgot my manners. My name is Tasira. It is a pleasure to meet you Batah." Tasira answered formally.

"The pleasure is mine, Tasira. What may I help you learn today?" Batah asked.

Tasira thought for a moment and then an important question entered her mind. It was something neither her mother or father had ever answered. She looked at Batah and asked.

"Why can't all Tuulans have female children like my mother. She has a medallion to help her. But why do the Tuulans have only male children?" Tasira looked at Batah, confused.

Batah looked at Tasira as if she were gauging the young girl's ability to understand such an adult question. After a short pause, Batah nodded and gave her an answer.

"Do you see the book that is twinkling?" Tasira nodded. Batah nodded back. "Please pick it up and place it in the viewer." Tasira picked up the glowing jewel and looked around.

"What is a viewer, Batah?" she asked. Batah motioned to a small indentation in the wall.

"When you place the book in the indentation and hold the palm of your hand over it, the book will reveal its contents into your thoughts. Within minutes you will understand all of the information held within it." Tasira nodded and placed the jewel in the indentation.

"This won't hurt, will it," she asked with raised eyebrows.

"No, I will not let anything hurt you. I promise."

Tasira hesitantly placed her hand on the jewel and a flood of images went through her mind. It was like seeing a memory from someone else's mind. She saw the genetic testing and the gender choosing and the awful pride that caused this to happen. She saw everything, including the tossing of unwanted infants to die outside the wall of the Outlands. Her head started to spin and she felt a little sick to her stomach. Batah looked at the young girl who had just been shown the knowledge of an adult.

"This knowledge is a terrible part of the Tuulan history. We created babies that were male, to satisfy the pride of the parents. The parents often did not want the female children, so they cast them beyond the barrier to die.

The Elders of that time controlled the birth of infants. By the Law of Tuulan Heritage Protection. Only genetically perfect babies were allowed to survive. Any imperfection, and the child was cast into the Outland like rubbish. Even the birth of a female child could be deemed genetically flawed. It was thought that only males could carry on a family name and bring honor."

"This is why Tuulans do not have female babies. With each genetic alteration, the entire population suffered. It was not a swift change, but a permanent one I am sorry to say." Batah finished her explanation and looked at Tasira again.

"Do you have another question for me?" Tasira looked pale and felt a little queasy, but she continued on with her quest for knowledge.

"Can you show me what happened to the babies that were thrown outside the wall?" she asked Batah.

"Of course, but are you sure you want to have this knowledge?" Batah asked. Tasira closed her eyes and nodded.

"The first thing I will show you is not in one of the books, but in a picture. You laid down the document I wish you to see. It is the top drawing." Batah waited until Tasira picked up the document.

"This is a map of the city and the Outlands. I, myself, used the library to create these images. I am afraid that they are not completely accurate. It is difficult for me to understand the limits of a two-dimensional drawing, but I knew that someday I would be able to find someone who could. I am glad that it is you, Tasira. You will need this information to complete your quest." Tasira looked at Batah, confused.

"What quest?" Tasira asked.

"When you have finished gaining the knowledge of the ancient texts, you will understand. Do you wish to continue today, Tasira?"

"Have the suns set, Batah? I must go home before they hit the horizon."

"Then you will have to continue another day. The suns are just beginning to set upon the sands. Remember, you were the one this place revealed itself to, and it must be you who keeps its secret. Do not forget you must complete your education. And by the growing anger I feel on this planet, it had best be soon." Batah finished ominously.

Tasira ran the entire distance to the other side of her home. She made it on time...barely. She looked down into the basket of her things and she found an item that she had never seen before. Batah must have placed it in there when she had her eyes closed. But how? Batah could not pick up any of the items she wanted Tasira to study. It was very odd, but she knew she was meant to show this to her mother and father. If it was in the basket, there must be a reason to have it discovered.

"I see you have returned from the castle." Caleb smiled and then turned stern. "I also see that you are out of breath from running so you could make it back for the evening meal." He raised his eyebrows, "You need to make sure you are on time every evening. Your parents have much to worry about without having to go searching for you."

Tasira looked down at the floor, knowing that Caleb was right. She had heard the terrible things that were on the paper Tam had retrieved. Mother didn't need anything else to worry her.

"I am sorry Uncle Caleb, I will try to be more responsible," Tasira stated in an adult tone. Caleb stopped chopping the fruit he was readying for the evening meal and looked strangely at Tasira. There was something different in her tone the evening. He nodded at the young girl and watch her put her things away. Everything except for a piece of strange looking paper.

"What did you find Tasira?" Caleb asked.

"I found this today in the old part of the house and I wanted to show it to Mother and Father. I don't know what it is, but maybe it will cheer them up a bit." Tasira shrugged, knowing she would have to find a way to keep her secret with Batah without actually lying to her parents. She had never lied to them before and she was not going to start now.

"May I see it?" Caleb asked.

"Of course, Uncle Caleb. I do not understand the strange markings on the paper. Maybe you can help me understand it." Tasira opened the strange, folded paper and showed it to Caleb.

"Do you know what the markings mean? I have studied Tuulan writing in school, but this isn't like the words I learned to write." Caleb wiped his hands and took the paper from Tasira's hand. She was right, there was some kind of strange writing on the paper along with some drawings.

"Come along Tasira, we are going to talk to your Mother and Father. They are in the Great Hall with the rest of the men." Caleb grabbed the young girl's hand and practically drug her into the Great Hall. She struggled to keep up with Caleb's long stride.

Chapter Nine

Nathan and Mara were talking to Pel and Tam when they heard the heavy footsteps walking toward them. Everyone, including the four discussing the latest problem, looked at Caleb dragging little Tasira behind him. Caleb was usually so gentle with the children, but something was so important that he forgot how small Tasira was. To say it was odd would be an understatement.

"Nathan...Mara, you must look at the paper Tasira found in the old wing. I can understand some of it, but the rest is a puzzle to me." Caleb stated excitedly. Nathan looked at the paper, and then to his smallest offspring.

"Where did you find this, Tasira?" Nathan asked as he took the paper from Caleb. It felt odd in his hands, like no paper he had ever held before. He unfolded it and looked at the odd writing. He looked towards his grandfather, Ket, and asked, "Do you know how to read this?"

"I, also, can only make out a few of the words," he motioned to Pel. Pel was the oldest of their clan, he had been born in the ships that had brought the Tuulans to Earth. He was over 600 years old and nearing the end of his life. Ket brought the paper over to the old Tuulan and handed it carefully to him. Pel looked at the paper for a long time, stopping to think occasionally while staring vacantly at the ceiling. After what seemed to be hours, Pel spoke.

"It is a story which is written in a combination of the Ancient, Middle and present forms of the Tuulan language. I believe this was done to ensure that an elder, of Tuulan blood, would be the one to read it. It is the story of the female known as Kala, the archeologist who found the glowing stone that makes the medallions our people hold as sacred. The stone was deep in the heart of Tuulani and was made of two distinct halves that made the stone whole. This describes where the male and female medallions come from and it is why they are similar, yet very different. The entire stone was brought up to the surface to make the medallions. One set for the men and one set for the women. The power of the stone was not completely known until much later in our history." Pel continued to read the story.

"The larger side of the stone was chosen to represent the male Tuulans and to give them strength against the warriors of Kuutarii. We were at war with them when Kala found the stone. Each of the ruling families received a set of medallions and the remaining stone was planted under the Hermes tree that covers the Hall of Elders today. It was also where the first Priestess was anointed by the elements of Tuulani.

"The Priestess resided in what was called "The Great Temple", just outside of the Hall of Elders. Her descendants remained there until the last female of her bloodline went in search of a race who could help us have female children once more. She left on one of the ships that went to Earth with the remaining women of Tuulani." Pel looked at Mara.

"That is the voyage to your planet, Mara. The remaining women were killed or died of old age in that voyage." All of the men looked at Mara.

"Do not worry, Mara. We do not blame you for this tragedy," stated Jonathan, smiling gently at Mara. Although he was one of the youngest men that came from Earth to Tuulani, he was one of the most compassionate as well. "Continue with the story, Pel," he stated to the old Tuulan. Pel nodded.

"The most powerful of these medallions was given to the Priestess who channeled all of the stone's power and created peace between Kuutarii and Tuulani, saving the remaining part of the planet from complete destruction. This is the city we live in today." Pel looked up at the others as he finished. "The bottom of the document has been smudged and I cannot read anything else."

Nathan looked at his daughter once again, "Where did you find this paper Tasira?"

"In a big room in the old wing," she said nonchalantly, shrugging her shoulders.

"There are many big rooms in the old wing, Tasira," her mother stated gently. "Which room was it? Try to think very hard Tasira, this is very important."

"I don't remember for sure, but this is all that I found in the staircase to bring home with me," she answered once again, trying to look as if it wasn't of much interest to her. But inside, her heart fluttered as if it had wings. She could barely wait until the next day to return to the library and Batah. "Can I go again tomorrow, Mother?"

"No, you can go back now...with me," Mara stated firmly. "Nathan, you should come along with us, don't you think?"

"Of course! We can look at the castle at night!" he said, trying to sound as playful as possible. Tasira wasn't falling for any of it. Something had changed in her young mind today. She was growing, mentally, towards adulthood far before her time. For now, though, she would play along and show them around the old wing. Unless she asked the staircase to open, she knew they would never find it. Never the less, she was excited at the thought of returning.

"Let's have our evening meal first." Tasira stalled, needing time to calm herself. "I'm starving, mother. Can we eat first?"

Mara motioned for Caleb to help her to get the food on the table. The other men got the table ready and within fifteen minutes the evening meal had been hurriedly eaten. Mara looked at Nathan and nodded.

"Caleb, do you think we could clear the table and get the lanterns ready for an evening adventure?" Nathan asked. Caleb nodded and the others started cleaning the room as quickly as possible. Everyone was excited at the thought of Tasira leading her parents to more information. The story Pel read was the first written record of their ancient history. Most everything ancient had been destroyed in the war with Kuutarii. The sacred knowledge of the planet had been lost and forgotten.

This document was something to cherish and the Tuulans were hungry for more stories of their ancestors.

A little over three hours later, Mara was getting tired. She and Tasira looked at every staircase and there was nothing more to find. In fact, Tasira wasn't even sure which staircase she had found it in. Many of the staircases had hidden doorways to another room, but there was nothing left but dust and a little girl's footprints.

"Can we go home now Mother?" Tasira asked as she yawned. Mara looked at Nathan and nodded.

"Yes, I suppose it is time for you to get to bed." Mara answered softly. She picked up the lanterns and Nathan scooped up the tired little one in his arms.

Tasira had been going to the old wing every day since they went on their evening adventure six months ago. Mara was glad that Tasira had found a place to feel safe and still be adventurous. But Tasira was not the child Mara had on her mind today.

Today, she and Nathan were to present themselves to the Hall of Elders. They were to bring Nathaniel and Qata with them and provide evidence that they were not holding Qata against her will. It should be a quick decision for the Elders to make, but Mara was feeling anxious about it. It was the kind of anxiety rush she used to feel when she knew she was going into a fight. The feeling had become well-honed while she was in the Patrol on Earth. It was strange to be feeling like that today.

"Good Morning, Mara," Qata stated brightly. She twirled around happily with her arms stretched out." It is going to be a glorious day! I just know it!" Mara smiled back at the happy young girl. It was so pleasant to have happiness surrounding her.

"Good Morning, Mother!" Nathaniel practically shouted as he came into the room. Mara raised her eyebrows at volume of the young man's booming voice. Nathan followed his son into the Great Hall shortly afterwards.

"Happy today?" Nathan smirked.

"Definitely happy, Father." Nathaniel looked at Qata. Qata nodded back. "Qata has agreed to be my mate. We wanted to tell you first before we petitioned the Hall of Elders." The young man looked back and forth between his Mother and Father. "Isn't that the most wonderful news?"

Nathan looked at his son and nodded with a smile. Then he looked at Mara, she was nodding and smiling too, but something was bothering her. He motioned to Mara to follow him into the foyer.

"What bothers you, Mara? Are you not happy about our son and Qata?" Nathan asked his wife. Nathan gathered Mara in his arms and looked down into her face. She laid her cheek against his chest and hugged his massive frame.

"I am happy for them, Nathan." She looked up into his face. "But it feels like there is something bad waiting for us today. I know all seems well, but I haven't had this kind of feeling since we were on Earth looking for the entrance to my grandfather's hiding place. We were almost captured by the Patrol." Mara placed her face down against his wide chest once more. "What if this isn't just a feeling? What if something bad happens and we cannot stop it this time?" Nathan rubbed Mara's back softly.

"Are you sure it's not the fear of what the Elders might say?" he asked in a quiet voice.

Mara nodded her head, "Perhaps that is it after all." But the pit of her stomach said otherwise.

Chapter Ten

Tamara had joined the other children in the play yard outside the school. U'na had just left and now Tamara was alone with the other children. Her mother would be very angry if she knew that she had been playing outside almost every day. Tamara was always very careful at judging her surroundings. Each escape route and alternate scenarios played out in her mind before she ever left the house.

"Your mama will be in big trouble today!" Foro smiled widely at Tamara. "My mama will win and you will be nothing but a servant. Maybe even my servant!" The little brat yelled at her. Tammy didn't even acknowledge his existence. That is, of course, until he and his friends threw rocks at her.

Tammy looked at the ground, trying to resist the temper that flared inside her. Her best friend Wynn looked at her with a fear of what she would do. She straightened up and went back to playing with the other girls that hadn't run away. She turned her back to Foro, insulting the boy's fragile ego.

"Hey, I am talking to you...you...you little half-breed...*du'lupa*!" He stammered out the insult. Tammy rolled her eyes at his pathetic attempt to goad her. "Can you not hear, *du'lupa*? Or maybe you are just stupid! Maybe even too stupid to be a servant." Foro laughed and a few of the other boys laughed as well.

"You are the stupid one, Foro. Can't you come up with your own insults? Or does Mama have to help you with that, too?" With that said, she turned her back once again. This time Foro could not resist the urge to show Tammy that he was superior to her.

Foro came up behind Tammy and drew out his claws. He was too young to have the nails of an adult Kuutaran, but he could still do considerable damage. Foro raised his hand and made a sweeping arc across Tamara's back causing deep gashes in her shoulders and spine.

The blow brought Tammy to her knees. She took a deep breath and stood up, turning around slowly as she rose. Her back was bloody and her shirt torn. As she stood there looking at Foro, she made a calculated effort to determine the best course of action.

"Are you looking to die, Foro?" she asked in a slow, quiet voice. Foro just smirked at her, proud of his achievement with a false bravado. He looked around at the other male children, with his chin held up a little.

"I should be asking you that question. I was able to take the first strike and you could not stop me." he retorted, a self-satisfied look on his face.

"That is because I had my back turned. Only a fool with no honor would attack in such a manner." Tamara stopped for a moment and gathered her composure.

"I ask you again," she said in the same low voice, "do you want to die?"

Foro looked back at his "friends" who were slowly backing away from him. They kept going until they had joined the others who were watching with fear. Foro's face lost the smile quickly and the bravado was quickly replaced with a pale fear.

"You have no right to threaten me!" He yelled. "If you do anything to hurt me, your parents will have to bear the shame...again." Foro smiled in a half-crazed state of mind. Tammy could see that the fear was seeping into the little brat's mind and controlling him. She looked at the ground once again, thought about her options, and raised her face to look at Foro with a smile. She motioned her friends to come over to her. They gathered in a small circle to listen to Tamara whisper her plan. Wynn stepped back with her eyebrows raised and ran towards her home.

"This is your last chance, Foro," Tammy stated in a condescending manner. "Are you willing to apologize and tell the Elders what has really happened," her smile faded. The look on her face now was ominous, "Or are you willing to die here and now?" she finished.

"A Kuutaran would never apologize to a half-breed Tuulan like you. You do not have the ability to kill me." Foro looked at Tammy and then to his friends.

"She is not able to carry out her threat," he motioned to Tamara. "This all a big lie."

Tammy lifted her eyes and saw Wynn behind Foro. She nodded to her and walked up to Foro as the other girl stood directly behind Foro. "Well, let's just see how unable I am, Foro."

As the words left her mouth, she quickly grabbed the Kuutaran by the arm, spun around him and grabbed the other arm. Tamara quickly took the braided rope from Wynn and tied Foro's wrists behind him, then dropped down to tie the boy's feet together. After that was completed, Tammy took off her outer shirt and gagged Foro with it. With this done, she looked at the other children.

"You will all come with me to the House of the Elders and tell the truth." She looked at each of them in the eye, "If you do not, I will deal with you separately. Follow me." Tamara stated. As quickly as she had tied Foro, she threw him over her shoulder and carried him into the city towards the Hall of Elders. The others walked with her, knowing that it was time for the bully Foro to pay for his actions.

D'kal, unaware of the procession heading up the back streets, was preparing her husband for the meeting at the Hall of Elders. Today she would crush the House of Nathan with lies and gain control of the city through the new Ra Shan, her husband Tavon.

"Now remember, dear husband, that we have been in mourning at the loss of our daughter, Qata. She has been taken against her will by Nathan and Mara and we have not seen her since. For all we know, she is dead." She paused for a moment and looked into Tavon's eyes. "We must convince the Elders by any means necessary. Do you understand?" she finished, agitated. Tavon looked at D'kal and nodded his head. Tavon walked toward a cabinet, took out a bottle of fine liquor, and took two long drinks. D'kal walked up to him and grabbed it from his hands.

"This has been your problem as long as I have known you. You cannot let this drink blur your focus from the meeting today. You are lucky that I was willing to do the bonding with you. This," and D'kal held up the bottle, "is the reason that you could not find a mate. You would be nothing if you did not have me by your side." D'kal finished harshly.

"I believe you were the desperate one, my love." Tavon sneered at D'kal. "You have gotten much more from this alliance than I have. I did not need to have a mate. I could have continued to visit Kuutarii and found a thousand more whores like you." Tavon chuckled. "No, my love, you are the fortunate one. I was just a drunken Tuulan who found a willing whore to bond with me." D'kal slapped his face.

"Do not think for one moment that I could not have found another. I just wanted to find a Tuulan who would be able to give me the power that your name gives." D'kal narrowed her eyes.

"I am the reason that you will become Ra Shan. You needed a female with the ability to think ahead and plan, and I was the perfect match."

"What you do is manipulate, not plan. But it does not matter, I have made my choice. I will never know happiness I may have had with another. That is the price

I pay for bonding with you." With that said, Tavon continued to finish practicing what he would say at the Hall of Elders. There is almost nothing Tavon would not do for D'kal. The bonding stone had trapped him in a one-sided relationship and he was doomed to love her.

Chapter Eleven

Tasira had left to go to the library and was talking to Batah about the meeting with the Elders. There was only one book left and Batah had told her she must watch it. It was the final truth she must know and understand.

Batah had shown Tasira many historical documents and books. The second book was about the genetic manipulation that took place. Tasira saw the scientist and doctors make changes to the cells and then place the child in the mother's womb. This went on for centuries until the male children outnumbered the female children by five times. By then it was too late, the population was destined to die out for the want of a perfect male. It was all about power.

The next century brought the war and most of Tuulani was destroyed. The knowledge of the books was tucked away. Every elder Tuulan with the knowledge of genetics was captured. Tasira could see the torture they endured by the Kuutaran soldiers before they were killed. Tasira vomited after viewing that book.

Next was a tour of the "under-house" and the path of each tunnel. Tasira was given a map of the tunnels and shown how to get back and forth from her bedroom to the library. Batah had also shown her how to get to the Hall of Elders and the Hall of Records within it.

"It is now time for you to see the last book. It hasn't been viewed in over six hundred years." She showed Tasira the glowing stone. It wasn't shaped like the others. The silhouette was smooth and tapered on the bottom like the others, but on top was a small spire.

"Will this one hurt?" Tasira asked, her green eyes looking directly at Batah.

"Yes, little one, this one must pierce your hand to give you the full knowledge of the book," Batah said in a factual manner. "You must decide now. The book will not reveal itself to you unless you understand the risk."

"Risk?" Tasira asked. Batah nodded at her.

"By letting the book become one with you, you risk knowing things that may be too much for your mind to withstand. It could kill you if your mind tries to block the pain that comes with the knowledge. This is why no one has viewed this book in so long." Batah looked at the young girl, "You must make this decision alone."

"I will view the book, Batah." Tasira nodded, knowing that this could be the last piece of information she would need to help her family.

"Take the stone and place it in the viewer. Once that is complete, position your hand over the stone." Batah instructed. She watched as Tasira complete the tasks and then pointed to the carved stone above the viewer. "Take this stone and place it on top of your hand. When the viewing begins you will have to fight to stay conscious."

Tasira did as Batah instructed. When the stone was on top of her hand, it became so heavy that she could not move it.

"It is like a thousand stones are keeping me from moving my hand." Tasira said to Batah in wonderment. At the same moment, the spire pierced her hand and she cried out.

The images were flying across her brain so quickly that she had to close her eyes. The next flurry of images brought the young girl to her knees, her hand held tight above her. The third and last level of images came to her even faster, imbedding themselves in her subconscious and conscious mind. The knowledge burned like the suns were peering at her very core, but she refused to give in to the pain. A few moments later, the stone released itself. Tasira opened her eyes and looked at Batah.

"There is much I must do to prepare for my journey." Tasira stated simply. "I must go and collect my supplies. This is the right time to leave. My parents will be distracted by the proceedings at the Hall of Elders." Tasira stopped and looked at Batah.

"I am glad that I found you and this library. When I return, I will share the knowledge with everyone. Thank you, Batah. Now I understand." With that said, Tasira grabbed the map, and looked once more at her friend Batah. She could not tell anyone of her quest. It would be too dangerous.

"Travel along the path the book has shown to you. There are small resting places like the oasis at the edge of the City. Use this knowledge to your advantage. May Tuulani care for you on your journey." Batah said and then disappeared into the nothingness once again. As Tasira watched her friend disappear, she grabbed her bag went to her home to gather the things she would need.

Tasira watched her parents dress for their appearance at the Hall of Elders. Mother was wearing the dress that she had gotten so long ago on Earth. Father was wearing the new shirt that Mother had made for him.

"Nathan, what should I do about the medallion?" Mara asked nervously. Nathan rubbed his forehead.

"I think that you should leave it here until we know what the Elders will say."

"I will put it back until we know for sure," Mara nodded.

Tasira watched her mother place the medallion in its hiding spot under their mattress. Tasira did not know that there was another who watched her mother also, wanting the same thing that she did. Only the reasons were different.

Tasira crept down the hidden stairs behind the wall of her parent's bedroom. She opened the small door quietly and ran over to grab the box with the medallion.

As she was retrieving her prize, she heard something outside the door. Tasira quickly rolled under the bed and listened as the door quietly opened and shut. She could hear footsteps coming toward the bed and saw a pair of feet walk around the bed. *"I've got to get out of here. They will be looking under the bed next."* Tasira thought frantically. And then she remembered the tunnels. There was an entrance to the tunnels on the other side of the bed in the closet floor. It would be easy to access, but she would still have to be out in the open for a few moments. She thought for a few moments and then grabbed the edge of the cloth that had a lantern on top of it. Tasira pulled the cloth and the lantern fell off the bedside table and made a loud crash. The footsteps ran over to the lantern and Tasira took the time to move the three feet to the closet. She quickly opened the entrance panel to the tunnels and could hear the footsteps above her. Whoever that was, left very quickly as well.

Tasira gathered all of the supplies she would need for the journey. A large messenger bag was filled with food, a change of clothing, a few other items and the map. An over-sized water skin was filled and slung over the other shoulder. When she was satisfied that she was prepared, Tasira started walking down the longest tunnel. She arrived at the edge of the city and the sand wall in a very short time. Once there, she pushed the blue jewel on top of the large stone. As she did so, the wall parted and Tasira walked through the opening. She looked back and saw the archway closing behind her.

"There is no turning back," she thought as she started her journey into the Outlands. As she looked up, she could see nothing but the heat rising up from the sands that had no end. She folded the map and changed her course to match the path she needed to follow.

Chapter Twelve

Tamara and her entourage arrived at the Hall of Elders just before her parents, and, D'kal and Tavon arrived. She spoke to the old Tuulan sitting outside the building.

"We wish to speak to the Elders." Tamara stated in an adult voice. The old Tuulan nodded his head at Tamara.

"You may follow me into the foyer and I will go ask," he replied politely. A small smirk played at the corners of his mouth. Shortly afterward, a young male opened the Hall doors and invited them in to speak with the Elders. At the semi-circle table was the male Tamara had spoken to outside. He was sitting at the head position at the center of the table. Tamara closed her eyes in embarrassment and sighed. This was not her day at all.

"You wished to speak to us, Tamara?" Jes asked. Tamara looked up at him in amazement. "Oh, yes, we know who you are. We make a point of knowing everyone in the city. It makes understanding the nature of the request much easier." Again, the old man smirked at Tamara. "But please, tell us why you needed to speak to us." All eyes at the table turned to her.

Tamara threw Foro off her shoulder and laid him carefully at her feet. The rest of the children stayed at the door of the Hall and were watching Tammy's every move. She motioned for the rest of them to come in and stand by her. They cautiously did as they were told and looked at the Elders fearfully.

"This boy, Foro, from the House of Tavon, harmed me in an unprovoked manner." Tamara stated. "Foro has done this before. He harmed my sister, Tasira, and I punched him in the face." She looked down for a moment. "I know now that I should not have hit him. It was not the honorable thing to do." Tammy turned around to show the Elders the deep gouges on her back and the bloody remnants of her undershirt.

"He did to me today. This time I did not hit him or harm him in any way other than tie him to ensure he would face you, and follow the decision you make. He should not be allowed to do this to another in the future." Tammy finished.

"Tamara, please untie the boy and take the shirt out of his mouth," stated Jes. Tammy did what she was told and soon the Kuutaran boy was on his feet.

"You will pay for this, you filthy half-breed. They will see you for what you are!" he yelled.

"That will be enough, boy!" Jes pounded a gavel and looked to the other Elders. "Each child tell us their version of events." He looked over at the young Tuulan male that had led Tamara and the others into the Hall. "Close the doors and let no one in until we have heard all of them."

One by one they each told their stories to the Elders, each Elder at the table asking questions until they had heard the full story. This went on for hours and everyone who was scheduled to speak at the Hall of Elders was told that they could wait in the foyer or come back another day. Tavon and Nathan were told to wait since the Elders wished to speak to them next.

Nathan, Mara, Nathaniel and Qata sat on the left side of the foyer and Tavon and D'kal sat on the right. The only sound was D'kal rubbing her long nails together until the large doors of the Hall of Elders started to open.

First out of the door was Foro. He was crying. He saw his mother and ran over to her. The rest of the children filed out silently and the last one out of the door was Tamara.

"Tamara!" Mara cried out. Tammy walked over to her mother and winced slightly when Mara hugged her. "Tammy, what is wrong?" Mara asked. Tamara turned around and showed her back to her mother. Mara gasped.

"It is nothing mother." Tammy said nonchalantly. "The Elders wish to speak to you and the others in the Hall." She grabbed her mother's hand. "Come with me and I will show you," she stated with a smile.

D'kal walked up to Tamara quickly and raised her hand to slap her. This time it was Tamara who caught her wrist.

"I will not let you hit me, D'kal. I have no wish to fight you, unless you force me to defend myself." Tamara stated plainly. D'kal lowered her hand, realizing what she had almost done in the Hall of Elders. It would have been an appalling display.

They all walked in together toward the table in the Hall. Jes stared at them sternly as they came closer. The intensity of the stares of the entire group weighed heavily on them all.

"Do you realize what has happened today, Tavon?" Asked Jes. "How about you, Nathan?" Both men shook their heads. Jes took a deep breath and sighed.

"I imagine you two have been so intent on the bid for Ra Shan that you have forgotten your most sacred duty. Your duty to be fathers and keep your children safe...even when they think they are old enough to act as adults." Jes looked at Nathan and then his gaze fell on Tavon.

"You are no father at all if you let your child hurt another. Not once, but at least twice." The old male stared at Tavon, boring through him with intense disapproval. Jes looked at Tamara and smiled a little, seemingly proud of the young woman's actions. Then he looked at Nathan and Mara.

"You have a remarkable young woman on your hands. She is strong and honorable. She tells the truth...even when it not what you want to hear. She was the leader of most of the city's young citizens today." Jes looked at the other Elders, they nodded their approval for him to be their voice today. Jes looked at Tavon and D'kal.

"You, on the other hand have raised a young man who is petty and seeks power." Jes looked directly at D'kal.

"I see that this has been nurtured in him." He stared at D'kal for a few moments and then swept his hand in a manner suggesting that she was not worthy of his time. He stared again at Tavon.

"Your child maliciously harmed another child today. The child he struck did not strike back. Instead she tried to ignore him." He stood up and leaned over the table with his hands spread wide and flat. The effect was impressive as he attempted to make his point.

"Your child will have to pay for this crime." Jes finished. This made D'kal speak up.

"That Human half-breed would say anything to gain your trust. I would not be so quick to judge my child if I were you," she finished with a sneer.

"You D'kal will sit down and be quiet before I have you removed! I have listened to the testimony of fifteen young Tuulans today and the combined voice says that your child is a troublemaker who likes nothing more than to use his father's power to get what he wants. He incites others to be cruel." Jes spoke in a booming voice that echoed throughout the Hall.

"Your son will have to take care of the House of Nathan for an entire month, in whatever capacity Tamara sees as appropriate. In addition, your house will have to give Tamara new clothing to replace the ones your son damaged." Jes finished and then looked at Nathan and Mara.

"You two will be responsible for ensuring that Tamara is properly trained and remains a truthful young woman. She has already stated that she would like to be the attendant at the front doors of the Hall of Elders." Jes finished, smiling at Tamara. "If she continues to progress as she has so far, the job should not be difficult."

"I know you have come here today expecting a different kind of decision to be made, but that will have to wait for another month...at the soonest. One problem at a time... one problem at a time." Jes said as he and the other Elders left the Hall.

Later that evening, D'kal got a visitor at her bedroom window. "I have seen the locket. Mara hides it under her bed, but I did not have time to get it. Someone was coming. A lantern had fallen and had make a loud crash," the visitor stated in a whining voice. A loud crack echoed in the still evening air as D'kal slapped the visitor's face.

"I need that medallion and you know why." D'kal whispered harshly. "You had better get it for me or our agreement is off. Now go!" The visitor nodded and left with a red impression of D'kal's hand on the right cheek.

MIRAGE IN THE SAND

Chapter Thirteen

Tasira had been walking for a number of hours now and she sat down for a moment in the cool of the night. She looked at the rations and chose to eat only a half of a honey biscuit with a bite of dried meat tonight. She would have to be frugal in order to stretch the big bag of food for a lengthy trek. If she ate just enough to stave off the hunger and to keep her energy level, she should have enough for a couple of weeks. By then, she should have reached her destination.

In the darkness she heard the howl of a ze'ev in the distance. It made her a little nervous, but she knew that she would be safe. Tasira pulled the medallion out of its soft bag and laid it on the sand. She closed her eyes and spoke the words the last book had taught her. The medallion glowed brightly and then darkened. She placed the medallion around her neck and promptly fell asleep.

Tasira woke to the two suns rising across the sands. She placed a light cloth over her head and walked until she found a large rock. It had taken until the suns were high above her to find the rock. She quickly made a makeshift awning and rested under it until the suns became low on the horizon. Her rest seemed to fleet by too fast.

"Well...I had best start out again," Tasira said to the suns. She took a large gulp of water and ate the other half of her biscuit. She thought of her parents and worried for them. By now they would be searching for her. She also felt the presence of something out there on the sands. Something she could not see. She grabbed the knife her mother had given her when she had been attacked. She looked at the knife and marveled at how long ago that day seemed. She rolled that memory through her mind as she collected her supplies.

Mara and Nathan hadn't looked for Tasira immediately after returning from the Hall of Elders. They had been so proud of Tamara that they didn't notice that not all of the family was not there. Mara had gotten the twins and they listened to Tamara tell the story while Pel tended to the wounds on her back. Everyone was so happy that Tamara was going to be the attendant at the Hall of Elders. The time ticked away and it was late that night when they noticed that Tasira had not come back from her castle.

At first Mara was mad at Tasira for not returning on time. The whole family came along and helped to search the old wing. After a couple of hours, they knew that Tasira was not in the house. Mara began to worry, but she said she was going to give Tasira some time to come home. Maybe she had fallen asleep somewhere they hadn't looked. But Tasira was not still not home the next morning.

"Nathan, what are we going to do? She has been missing for more than a day." Mara cried, tears falling openly. This was a rare show of panic from the strong woman. Nathan held Mara and she calmed down. She wiped her tears and stated in a strong voice, "We have to go to the Elders. What if she has been taken?"

"We will go now and ask for their help," Nathan nodded. He was worried about his wife, the move to this planet, the tension that the feud between Tavon and himself caused and now this. He had never seen her this distracted before. She was usually in control and charging into the fight.

The entire House of Nathan went to the Hall of Elders to ask for help in this emergency. The attendant told them to come into the foyer and wait. They became more nervous each passing hour. Maybe the Elders weren't going to talk with them today.

The large doors finally opened and the House of Nathan watched the House of Tavon walk out of the chambers. Tavon wouldn't look at them or recognize their presence. D'kal though, gave them a look that was pure hatred. They walked past and Foro followed closely behind his mother, head down and not acknowledging anyone.

"Do you think this has something to do with Tasira?" She looked at Nathan with worry.

"I am sure that this is just a coincidence, my love," Nathan said in a soothing voice as he held Mara's hand. But truthfully, he too was worried about the "coincidence".

"You may come into the Hall to speak with the Elders. They are ready to listen to your request," stated the young Tuulan as he opened the large doors.

The Elders sat in the same positions as they had before. Jes was at the center and watched them closely as they arrived. He motioned for them to sit down. All except Mara. He motioned her to come closer to the table.

"What is it you need, Mara?" Jes asked gently. The effect on Mara was immediate. She clasped her hands together and looked down at the floor, trying not to weep again.

"My daughter, Tasira, is missing. She has been gone for more than a day and we worry she may have been injured or taken from us and we want her to come home." Mara said in a rush of words. Jes looked at her inquisitively. The Mara he met when she came to this planet was not the woman he saw before him now.

"You have looked in every place possible?" Jes asked, out of formality. Mara nodded. "Well, then we shall ask Batah, the keeper of the city. If your daughter is in any of the public places, Batah will know." Jes got up from his seat and went to the statue of the priestess. He pushed on one of the jewels on the statue's belt. As he did so, the strange visage Nathan had seen so long ago, appeared before them.

"How may I help you?" Batah asked in a polite voice. Jes cleared his throat and motioned for Mara to ask Batah a question.

"I cannot find my daughter Tasira. Can you help me find her?" Mara asked as tears fell down her face. "I need her to come home and be safe." Batah looked at

Mara, and paused as if she were making a search of the city.

"I do not know where she is, Mara," the visage stated in a matter calm manner. "I cannot find her in any of the public places that I am allowed to search. I cannot search more intensely. Invading another's privacy is not allowed.

"Is there a way for us to look in another's house? I fear that my daughter has been kidnapped and is being held against her will." Jes looked sternly at her, knowing that she was thinking about D'kal.

"I am afraid not. You have also had this charge against your House." Jes stated. "The answer is the same for you as it is for anyone. You did not have your home searched, did you? Unless someone knows for certain that another has committed a crime, the Elders will not order the search of a home."

"What else can we do, Jes? My daughter is missing and we need to find her! She is too young and frail to be left on her own!" Mara looked at Jes beseechingly. Jes nodded and then looked down at the floor, rubbing his chin.

"Let us talk about this and we will send someone to your home when we have decided on the best course of action." Jes and the other elders stood up and left through the door to their chambers.

Nathan looked at Mara and stood up, hold his hand out for her. They clasped hands and started walking back home. The entire family left in silence and did not speak on the way

home.

Chapter Fourteen

Tasira looked at the roll of multiple documents in her hand. It was the middle of the day and it was time for her to rest again. But something was nagging at her in the back of her mind. She knew that if she concentrated hard enough that she might remember something or connect the two thoughts together to solve the riddle in the back of her mind. Maybe. *"But what do I concentrate on? I don't know where to start."* Tasira thought to herself. *"Maybe if I look at all of the documents again, I'll be able to figure it out."* She took the old parchments out of the old map case she had strapped over her shoulder.

She unrolled them and the first document was the map she had been using. It was fairly accurate and she seemed to be able to find the landmarks of stones and cliffs well enough. She had only needed to backtrack once. All things considered, Batah had done well to give her this. Tasira carefully rolled it up and placed it to the side.

The next document was written in the old Tuulan language and, although Tasira had studied the language with Batah, she was still having some difficulty in understanding it.

"The children of the Katolae Tuulans are most often born with a condition that renders them either unhealthy or visually offensive to society. These infants are to be given extract of the diru plant. The extract will hasten death, leaving the child to slowly drift into a permanent sleep. Once this process is completed, the death marchers will deliver the child to the Outlands where he or she will become food for the ze'ev. This will complete the circle of life from conception to death and will keep the society in harmony. It is the responsibility of all child bearing females to understand and accept this process. Any mother who does not follow the guidelines given to her by the Elders will be banished to the Outlands as well."

Every time Tasira read the ancient law, she wanted to vomit. How could they be so barbaric? Didn't they have any feelings for the children, or their parents?

Even after reading the disturbing paper, Tasira became sleepy. She had walked many days into the Outlands and her body was exhausted. Her eyes fluttered shut and she was soon fast asleep. Disturbing nightmares crowded into her repose, as they often did since she left the city. Very few rest periods were calm and secure, but this night was especially terrorizing.

In her dream she was standing back, watching a female Tuulan give birth. The young woman was excited to see her new arrival. She looked up at the doctor and his face was distraught, conveying without words the disappointment she would have to bear. He showed her a completely normal female child whose only deformity was a birthmark on her face.

The mother waved away the child, not wanting to look at her any longer. The doctor nodded and prepared the diru extract. Tasira was screaming at the top of her lungs for him to stop, but no one could hear her. The child was given the medicine and she slowly closed her eyes, her breathing became shallower.

A young male Tuulan came into the room and took the small child into his arms and walked out the door. Tasira's dream followed the child to the barrier where the young man opened the archway and walked out into the Outlands. He laid the child on the sand, said a quick prayer, and then used a small device to open the archway from the outside. Tasira was sweating when she awoke.

She looked around, half expecting to see someone, but all she saw were the two suns low over the horizon.

She got up and gathered her things. She started to roll the documents and then abruptly stopped. The thought nagging at the back of her mind finally reached her conscious mind. Her eyes flew open further.

Were there any mothers who refused to do this horrible act? If so, what happened to them? Batah had said that the rest of the knowledge she needed would be outside the barrier. With a renewed sense of purpose, Tasira prepared to leave. She walked for only a couple of hours when she could see that there was a strange darkness on the sands in the far distance. Tasira squinted and looked harder at the darkness and assumed it was her first glimpse of land other than the desert. She continued on toward the object and then suddenly stopped. Her keen sense of hearing was picking up a sound.

She stood there for a while just listening. Soon she continued on her way, telling herself that she was imagining things until she heard the sound again. This time it was louder and closer. She slowly turned around until she saw a large ze'ev coming at her.

Chapter Fifteen

The beast was covered in long thin fur and had deep golden flashing eyes in the moonlight. The snout was moving, both growling and sniffing the air around it. As it moved closer, it bared its large, dirty looking teeth. It circled around Tasira, making her turn to keep it in her sight. She did not want the ze'ev to think it had an advantage. She had heard stories that a ze'ev would not waste its' time to kill you before eating you as its dinner. There would be screams of agony, but no one would be around to hear you.

Tasira refused to let the old stories mark her fate. She placed a hand out as if to pet the animal. It took offense and lunged at her.

As the ze'ev's powerful body pushed forward, the medallion lit up as bright as the midday suns. The animal pulled back and began to whine. Tasira raised her eyebrows and smiled a little. She placed a hand around the medallion and then stretched out her hand, once more, toward the wolf-like animal. The ze'ev crouched down and growled a bit. It whined louder as Tasira's hand inched forward.

Soon, Tasira reached out completely and touched the wolf-dog on the head. As she did so, the medallion grew a little brighter.

"Good boy," Tasira said softly. "You and I are going to be best friends, aren't we?" She petted the animal's head some more. "You should walk with me on my quest. I think we could both use the company, don't you?" Tasira watched as the dog wagged its long straggly tail and moved in closer by Tasira.

As it came closer, the medallion flashed a little bit brighter and the glowing light encompassed both Tasira and the dog. She could feel the tension leave both her and her new best friend. She kneeled on the ground and the dog came up and licked at her face.

"Yes, I like you too, but you really need to do something about your breath. It smells as bad as week old garbage. Phew!" Tasira exclaimed. She took out one of the precious biscuits and gave half to the dog. It ate it as if it hadn't eaten in weeks. It probably hadn't. There was very little to fill the stomach of a ze'ev out on the sands.

"I think you need a name." Tasira took the challenge seriously. It had to be the right name to make a perfect fit. She thought for a minute and then smiled.

"I think you should be called Tinku. It is the name of a fighter!" She bent over and scratched the dog's ears. It laid down in the sand and rolled over on its back in a submissive pose. Tasira raised her eyebrows a little and laughed, "Although you don't look too aggressive now!"

Tasira picked up her things and called for Tinku to follow. The two of them continued on their way in the cool of the darkness. They walked side by side in the never-ending sand, noiselessly pushing forward to Tasira's goal.

Nathan could see Nathaniel and Qata kissing in the garden. He smiled, thinking back to the first time he and Mara had met. He had been in a pit and unable to get out by himself. She and her horse pulled him out, not knowing how he would react. She had been so brave, but now, he barely recognized that same woman.

Something was changing in Mara. She was becoming an emotional wreck and had even given up on her morning defense practice. He knew that he would have to make time to talk to her. Mara had always been a strong and reckless spirit who could handle almost anything, but she had been steadily changing since she arrived on Tuulani. The loss of their daughter, Tasira, seemed to hasten the transformation.

Mara came into the room where Nathan was watching the young couple in the garden. She smiled at the two kissing outside and then looked at her mate. He wasn't really watching them any longer. He seemed deep in thought.

"Good morning, Nathan," Mara said brightly. Nathan shook himself a little and turned around to see his wife. She was wearing the dress she had gotten while still on Earth.

"Good morning, my love." Nathan looked at her for a moment. "I was thinking of having a picnic for just the two of us. We can just pack the food now and find a quiet spot out by the oasis. What do you think? Shall we go?"

"I don't see why not, as long as we can find someone to watch the children." She stopped and looked outside again. The Elders had visited the House of Tavon, and reported that their daughter was not in the home. It was if she had just disappeared into the air. It was now over a month since Tasira had gone missing. Nathan had no answers and neither did she.

"Let's go and find one of the men and ask them to care for the children for a few hours," Nathan nudged her along toward the kitchen. After they had packed the food and Jonathan had agreed to care for the children, Nathan looked at Mara.

"I think you should go and change your clothing, Mara. You will burn in the sunshine if you are not properly covered." Nathan stated simply. "I will finish packing food and water while you change, OK?" Mara nodded and started up the stairs to their bedroom.

Mara knew that Nathan was trying to distract her from her sadness, but the only thing that would help her would be finding her smallest daughter. Tasira was so vulnerable. The thought of what may have happened to her weighed heavily on Mara's mind.

She changed into her black Patrol uniform and started to leave the room. She turned around and retrieved the box that held the woman's medallion, shoving it into one of her side pockets. It made her feel a little better knowing that she had the medallion with her. With that, she went down the stairs to find Nathan.

Chapter Sixteen

It took a short while to get to the oasis, but the walk was good for Mara. She slowly relaxed and began talking to Nathan about inane things until they were both smiling. It had been months since they had such a good time together.

Nathan had been busy with his bid to become Ra Shan, and Mara had drifted further away from him. But soon, they found a place under a tree to sit and enjoy their meal together. Nathan knew he needed to talk to Mara, but for right now, being in the company of just his wife was a rare treat. Mara was looking at him and smiling at him the way she did when they first met.

"I know that I shouldn't have brought this out of the house, but it always brings me peace when I wear it." Mara pulled the small, ornate box out of her pocket. "Should I put it on?" she smiled impishly.

"You know what happens when you and I are this close and I am wearing the medallion." She leaned over and kissed him. The kiss became more intense and soon they were laying naked, next to one another on the blanket. Mara reached over for the box. As she opened it, she realized that it was empty.

"Nathan, the medallion is gone!" She looked panicked. "Where could it be? I hid it the day we went to the Hall of Elders. The day Tammy was in trouble. I haven't worn it since."

"Let me take a look." Nathan took the box and spoke as calmly as he could. There was no reason to escalate her fears. He looked closer at the wooden cube he had made so long ago to hold the medallion. It was now lined with a fine fabric. He had not lined the box with anything.

"Mara, when did you line the box?" he asked his wife, puzzled. Mara blinked a couple of times trying to comprehend what he was asking.

"I didn't line the box with anything. It was perfect the way you made it. It needed nothing else. Why?" Mara completed the words anxiously.

"Get dressed. We are going to show this to the Elders before we take the lining out of the box. If there is anything unusual, we will want them present when we take it apart."

Mara nodded at Nathan and pulled on her uniform. They quickly packed up the lunch and ran towards the Hall of Elders. The Tuulans along the streets watched as they ran carrying the haphazardly packed basket and a small wooden box. Most of them went back to what they had been doing prior to seeing the couple, but some ran along behind. It seemed to Mara that it was taking much longer than it should to reach the Hall of Elders, but she was breathing too hard from running to ask Nathan.

At last, the large building with its shadowing Hermes tree was in front of them. Nathan was out of breath when he asked to see the Elders, but the young man showed them into the foyer as calm as ever.

Both Mara and Nathan sat down to catch their breath. It was only a short time before the large doors opened and they were welcomed into the Hall. The rest of the Tuulans who had followed them were sent home by the attendant. Jes, as always was seated at the center of the table.

"What brings you here today?" asked the old Tuulan. Nathan moved forward and pulled Mara with him.

"This does," Nathan answered, holding the small box in his hand. "This is the box where Mara keeps the medallion. When she opened it this morning, there was nothing in it. The medallion is gone." He heard all of the Elders gasp at this news. Mara's medallion was the only one of its kind and it held the future of Tuulani. Without it, the chance of the Tuulan race surviving for future generations would diminish. It could possibly erase the Tuulans from existence.

"This box has never had cloth lining. We wanted to take the box apart in your presence so that there would be no question of what we saw." Nathan looked up at Jes, "Do you want to be the one to take the box apart?"

"No," answered Jes. "We will watch you if you wish to take the box apart to look for clues. It is, after all, your property." Nathan nodded and looked again at Mara. Mara pulled out the small bladed dagger that she always wore with her uniform. Nathan stepped away and watched Mara carefully remove the fabric lining from the box. She loosened the fabric and removed it completely. Under the lining was a piece of Hermes paper. This made Mara gasp for she knew how highly the paper was prized by the Tuulans. Mara pulled out the folded parchment and held it out to Jes to read.

"No, Mara," he said gently, "It must be you who opens and reads this document. It must be very important though, for someone to have used the sacred paper."

Mara opened it very carefully, not wanting to look at the message until she could read it out loud to everyone present. Layer by layer she unfolded the document until it was a single sheet in front of her. She began to read aloud.

Mother,

I am sorry to have to leave you and Father so quickly, but I have been chosen to complete a quest. Batah has helped me research the books in the library and I have learned a great deal about our new home.

There were many terrible acts done by the people of Tuulani, on their own children, and I have been chosen to make this right. I have told Batah not to tell you of this quest until I am long gone. Do not be angry with her or me. We are trying to find peace for the remaining Tuulans.

Again, I am sorry to have left you without telling you why, until now. I also apologize for taking the medallion, but it is an essential item for this trip. There is so much more the medallion can do than create life. It will keep me safe. I will return as soon as possible. Please give this document to the Elders. I am hoping that it will become part of the official record as the first document of renewed peace. I love you Mother and Father.

Your daughter,

Tasira

The Elders and everyone else in the hall were completely silent. They all looked at one another in quiet astonishment. This continued for a few minutes until Jes stood up.

He walked over to the statue of the priestess and pushed the blue stone on her belt. Within seconds, Batah appeared in front of them.

"Batah, we have found the letter from Tasira. Do you know where she is?" Jes asked.

"She is on a quest," she stated.

"The letter tells us that much, Batah. Do you know, specifically, where she is at this moment?" Jes asked, a slight irritation to his voice.

"No, I do not know specifically where Tasira is at this moment," Batah cocked her head to one side to look at Jes. Jes looked skyward to stave off the need to kill the woman who was only a visage now.

"Batah, do you have a general idea of where the young female is at this time?" Jes asked, not caring that he was showing a considerable amount of vexation at Batah.

"No, I do not know," Batah answered. Jes walked away from Batah and was rubbing his face as he came closer to Mara.

"It is clear that the Keeper of the City has no knowledge to share with us at this point." Jes looked up at Nathan, "

You should take your mate home and help her look for other clues in your house. Perhaps the young woman left more information for you to find." Jes and the other Elders nodded and watched Nathan and Mara leave the Hall.

Chapter Seventeen

Tasira was snuggled up with her new friend under the awning she had created. That is to say that Tinku had decided to curl up next to her. She petted the ze'ev and they fell asleep under the protection she had made.

Soon, she was walking along the hot sand and found herself surrounded by large, twisted and marred Tuulans.

"What do you want of me?" Tasira asked.

"You!" the largest male yelled at her. His face was deformed and terrifying.

"Why do you need me?" Tasira answered back.

"You will come with us…or die right here on the sands," the large Tuulan smiled a crooked half smile at her. Tasira nodded her head and looked for Tinku. He was nowhere to be found. *"At least he will be safe,"* Tasira thought to herself.

The group of Tuulans brought her to the edge of the sands. They were now walking on green-blue grass. It was soft under her feet. She wanted to look at this marvel, but was prodded on by one of the Tuulans behind her.

"There is no need to be rude!" Tasira yelled. She thought for another moment and looked at the male behind her. She would try another tactic.

"What is your name," she asked in a sweet voice that made her teeth hurt. She did not like these kinds of games, but her mother had taught her that sometimes you must swallow your pride to get out of a bad circumstance. *"I'm pretty sure this is what you were trying to warn me about Mother."* she thought.

"My name is Qan. What is yours," he asked quietly. He looked at the others in front of them. Apparently, he was not supposed to be speaking to her.

"My name is Tasira," she whispered back to him. Perhaps she would have one ally. She smiled at him and he blushed as he smiled back.

The trip seemed to be taking hours, but soon they arrived at a primitive settlement that was surrounded by huge cliffs on three sides. In the center of the village was a large horn made from some type of animal's antler. *"It must be ancient. There are no animals this large,"* Tasira thought.

The horn was sounded and all of the residents of the village came out to see what the hunting party had brought back. They looked confused when they realized their catch was a female Tuulan.

At the very center of the group was a raised platform. An old male with a hunched back was climbing the stairs to the top. He motioned to the crowd to be silent.

"I am Ka'Le, the leader of this village. I am glad to see that the party has brought you back," he stated with a lopsided smile. "What is your name, female," his chin rising as he spoke.

"I am Tasira," she stated, her back straight.

"Well, well, Tasira," he smiled back. "We have two choices for you. You can become one of us, here in our village, to be available to all males as breeding stock. Or," Ka'Le paused for effect, "you can be served as one of the greatest evening meals we have had in a long time." He looked at Tasira again. "It is your choice."

"I will not be a slave to anyone," Tasira yelled. She grabbed for the medallion, but it was not there.

"It is of no matter to us." He motioned for Qan to come forward. "Kill her and have the females make ready to prepare a feast." Qan nodded. He leaned forward with his spear and plunged it into Tasira's heart. She could feel the blood splatter on her face as she screamed.

Tinku was licking Tasira's face as she awoke from the nightmare. She felt the sand underneath her and felt her chest. There was nothing there but the medallion. Tasira took a deep ragged breath and hugged Tinku. The dog whined a little and wagged its tail.

"Tinku, you are a good boy," Tasira said as she recovered from the nightmare. She took a deep breath and smiled at her companion. "I hope I never have another dream like that again." She continued to pet and talk to the ze'ev as she watched the suns drop lower on the horizon. She started to pack up her things and noticed how light the food and water had become.

"We had better make it to water by the end of tomorrow night or we will die out here Tinku."

Two more days had passed and Tasira was out of food and water rations. She was walking slower than before. Her body felt heavy and her lips were dry and cracking from the lack of moisture. The oasis that should have been part of her journey was no longer there. It had long dried up and her water skin had been dry since the day before. Tasira walked a few more hours and then collapsed on the sand.

Tinku lay next to her and howled. He licked at her face and tried to nudge her awake. Tasira looked at the ze'ev and raised a hand to pet him. The effort was too much and her hand dropped to the scorching sand.

SECRETS OF THE SANDS

Chapter Eighteen

"Tinku..." her voice trailed off. The dog perked his ears up and wagged his tail slightly. He stared at Tasira who lay unmoving and unresponsive. After he sniffed at her body a little, Tinku moved around to the opposite side of her and lay down in the path of the suns. He understood she needed to be cooled and shaded.

Tinku would not leave her now, as his nature should dictate. But, instead, he'd protect her against other ze'evs that may smell the taint of impending death on her.

It had been a couple of hours and Tasira had still not moved. The dog got up from his place next to her and walked around her body, sniffing as he moved. He could smell the difference in her body and looked around at the unending horizon. He put his nose up in the air and sniffed for any other threats to Tasira and then stopped. He raised his nose to the last direction he had sniffed and ran off as fast as his body could carry him.

He ran at full speed until he had reached a village. There were many people there and they just ignored him until he barked and ran up to an old woman and nipped at her hand. That got their attention. He would have help for his Tasira if he had to bite every one of them.

Nathaniel and Qata were at the Hall of Elders with the entire House of Nathan. The family had decided to list Tasira as dead on the scrolls of the city's census. She had been gone too long for her to have survived. It had been almost two years. Mara wept for her daughter, but knew that her son's bonding ceremony would help to ease some of the pain. She drew in a long breath and looked at Nathaniel and smiled.

Nathan held Mara's hand as she handed over the document that would list Tasira with the other Tuulans who had passed through the veil to the other side of life.

Tasira would live on there and would be happy once again. Mara took comfort in knowing that she would see Tasira again someday when she also passed through the veil. She smiled a little thinking of how her littlest child would once again be playing and happy in the other world. Mara thought of how much the twins, Telora and Ketasha, had grown since Tasira left. They were now bigger than Tasira would have ever grown. A tear ran down Mara's face as the document landed into Jes's hand.

As the document was handed over, Mara could hear loud voices coming from the foyer. The loudest voice she could identify immediately. It was D'kal. Yelling turned into a scuffle directly outside the large doors. Within minutes, D'kal, Tavon and Foro broke past the attendant and the doors flew open.

"You will stop this hideous blasphemy of a union between Qata and that mongrel Nathaniel. I will not allow it," Tavon yelled. He then looked a D'kal for approval. She nodded and pushed him slightly to continue. "My wife is overwrought with pain knowing that her daughter is marrying a male who is half Human."

"You have no right to tell me who I can bond with, *mother*," Qata ground out between her teeth. D'kal looked at Qata and smiled. It gave Mara a shiver down her spine. Something was not right.

"Do you really want to play this game, Qata?" D'kal said calmly as she looked down at her nails. "You should decide quickly before I become impatient," She smiled again, not looking up at Qata. It was apparent to everyone in the Hall of Elders that there was more to this than D'kal's being outraged at the bonding.

Qata looked at D'kal, "I wish to marry Nathaniel," she swallowed hard.

"Alright then. I have no other choice," she spoke as she pulled a document out of Tavon's jacket. "Thank you, darling," she patted his cheek as she retrieved the document. D'kal handed the document to Jes.

"No, don't open the paper. Please?" Qata looked beseechingly at Jes.

"He has to now, you stupid *kalbay*! I gave you a chance and you chose not to take my kind offer!" D'kal sneered at the young woman. "Now, you will pay the price!"

Jes opened the document and watched as the young Qata collapsed onto her knees. She had tears rolling down her face as she sobbed without sound. As he started to read the document, he raised his head and looked at the girl. Qata looked at him without saying a word, shaking her head slowly. Jes turned his attention to D'kal. His face was stern, with a frown and narrowed eyes.

"This document states that you purchased Qata from another family as if she were a piece of property."

Nathaniel sat down next to the crumpled Qata and held her against him.

"That is correct. Qata is my property and I want her back," D'kal smirked.

"This document is not valid here on Tuulani. We abolished this barbaric custom many millennia ago. Qata is a free woman on our planet. She may do as she wishes," Jes smiled at Qata.

"This is a valid document and I will have it upheld!" She spewed at Jes. "I am asking for a vote from The Council of Nine." D'kal gave Jes a haughty look, "It is my right as a citizen to ask for a vote."

"That is correct, D'kal," said Anda, the next eldest on the Council of Nine. "But we will hear the facts of the case before we render any judgment. Go and complete your statements and we will convene the Council of Nine when we are ready to do so." Jes nodded to Anda.

"Nothing brought to the Elders from either family will be completed today. Qata can stay at any home she wishes until the vote has been completed," stated Anda. He looked over to Mara and Nathan.

"This also means we will not be entering Tasira's passing into the scrolls. I am sorry." He nodded to the House of Nathan and all of the members that lived there.

Without another word, the Elders walked to the chamber, single file.

Chapter Nineteen

Tasira could feel her body floating along, not feeling anything. She tried to open her eyes, but she could only squint to look through her eyelashes. The suns were too bright. A large shadow passed over her face and she looked up again.

All she could see was a vague face far above her and a low, deep voice saying something she couldn't understand. She should've been afraid but she was too weak to care right now. She lost consciousness as she thought about the punishment of the suns and the family she would never see again.

The large man that was carrying her kept looking down at this beautiful, dark-haired woman. She was so light to carry that when others asked if he wanted to hand her to them so he could rest, he shook his head. He would continue to hold the woman in his arms as long as possible.

It had tried before to hold a female, but it never lasted very long. He could tell they were all afraid of him, and, he had long ago stopped hoping.

"Aziz, do you think this ze'ev is hers?" One of the men carrying the dog asked him. Aziz nodded at Gan.

"That dog ran for hours to find us and then led us back to her. I think it must love its master very much to risk its life. I never knew that a ze'ev could be tamed." Aziz looked down again at the small female. How could *she* have tamed a ze'ev? Ze'evs were aggressive and viciously fight for food. Aziz was dumbfounded. This female should be dead from the ze'ev's attack, not saved by the animal. He shook that thought out of his head and focused once again on the young woman he carried.

For the first time in many years, he daydreamed of having a woman he could have in his arms every day.

A few hours later, Tasira could feel the cool of the night surround her scorched body. Nothing had ever felt this wonderful. She opened her eyes and waited for them to adjust. Everything was blurry, but she could see green and blue and grey in front of her. She assumed she was close to death. The last thing she had seen was the never-ending sands of Tuulani. If this was going to be the end of her life, at least it was going to feel pleasant. Anything but the heat and thirst of the desert was a welcome change.

Tinku was laying by her side. She could feel his breath on her hand and his coarse hair. She petted him, thankful that she had such a devoted companion.

Tasira thought of all the knowledge she had gained from Batah. It was a shame that she would not be able to share it with anyone. She should have told Tammy about the library. At least she would've been able to pass along the vast stores of knowledge to someone else.

Now, unless the staircase chose someone new, it would be lost for another millennia. Maybe the Tuulans wouldn't survive that long without the medallion, she thought in shame. She wouldn't have taken it if she had known she would wind up lost somewhere on the sands.

Tasira continued to lay in the cool air and opened her eyes once more. Her sight was getting clearer and she could see more detail to the colors before her. She sat up, feeling weak and dizzy as she did so. She blinked again. She was most definitely not out in the desert any longer.

She could hear voices speaking in the background, but she could not understand all of the words. The old Tuulan dialect was not her strongest point, but she could tell that the voices were talking about her. She tried to stand up, but her knees were wobbly and she wound up back on the cot she had been laying on. She heard footsteps coming toward her and she pretended to be asleep.

"Te su'un se ka bakt Kala. Su'un te konu," the voice said as he walked away. She knew su'un was the word for woman and the name Kala was the name of the archeologist who had found the glowing stone. They were talking about the woman with the stone of Kala, in other words, they were referring to her. Maybe the rest was that she still had not awakened.

She let the footsteps walk away before she opened her eyes just wide enough to look through her eyelashes. She saw no one in the room, so she tried to get up once more. This time her body complied and she was walking along the wall for support. She needed to find out what kind of place this was before they caught her again. How did they find her? She didn't remember seeing any green grass before she collapsed.

Tasira walked into the darkness behind the building and peeked into the open archways where the cool air was allowed to blow in. There was a large Hermes tree a couple of hundred yards away from Tasira. She decided to use it to her advantage.

She walked as quickly as she could to the tree and climbed into the crook of its two large trunks. Tasira looked up and it made her a little dizzy. She was never the one to climb things. That was Tammy's specialty. Tasira was the one who would spend hours with books and read. She knew she was small and she never pushed herself to be anything other than what her family expected of her. She had learned some of the defense moves her mother taught her, but no more than was necessary. Now, she had no other choice. She would have to climb the tree herself.

"Ke su'un altan te?" A voice cut through the air. Apparently, her little escape had been discovered. Tasira jumped up and caught the first branch of the tree. Little by little she climbed toward the top until she found a place between two larger limbs that was almost completely covered by leaves. She looked around the small village and saw a young female in the center of the town.

Everyone else was searching for her, but the young woman turned around in a circle a number of times. As she turned around, arms out and palms up, she chanted, "Ke su'un, Tuulani? Ke su'un, Tuulani? Ke su'un Tuulani?"

Tasira realized that the woman was asking the planet to help her find Tasira. Now, when the woman turned around and faced Tasira, her medallion glowed slightly. As each circle was completed the medallion glowed a little more.

Soon, Tasira's medallion glowed like a beacon. It didn't take the rest of the village long to find her. She looked down and a large male was motioning for her to come down. Tasira shook her head, holding on to the tree even tighter. The large male looked at her again.

Chapter Twenty

"Ha'a, su'un!" The large man yelled, motioning for Tasira to come down. Tasira thought for a second and realized that getting down by herself would be a lot less dangerous that that hulk coming up after her. She looked down at the male and nodded. She started on her way down and grabbed smaller branches to balance herself as descended. One of the branches broke and in her weakened state she could not keep her balance. She fell, breaking branches on her way down. She landed into two massive arms as she reached the bottom. She looked up to see the smile on his face as she landed.

Aziz looked at the small Tuulan in his arms. He had thought he would never have the woman in his arms again. As he pulled leaves out of her hair, she slapped at his hand, her green eyes flashing. He couldn't help himself, he chuckled. That got more of the same from her. She said some words to him that he could not understand, but he was sure that they were not nice.

He smiled again and carried her over to their leader, Seta. As he placed her on her feet in front of Seta, the strange young female smacked him hard on the arm. Her chin went up and her tiny arms folded against her body. Aziz nodded once to Seta and then stepped back.

Seta raised her eyebrows at the fight in this young woman. She liked her even though her words did not mean anything to her. She motioned to Tasira to walk with her into the large building that looked remarkably like the Hall of Elders. Tasira looked around, the interior was beautiful.

"What is this place?" Tasira asked. The other woman looked at Tasira and shook her head. Tasira tried to say a couple of words in the old dialect.

"Ke hirsa?" Tasira sincerely hoped she hadn't said anything that was insulting. Seta looked at her, surprised.

"Ka bakt, Kala," Seta responded. Tasira was pretty sure she had said, "In the Holy place of Kala," but she couldn't be positive.

"Kala?" Tasira asked as she pointed to her medallion. "Te Kala Kumirta?" She was pretty sure that she asked if Kala was the Priestess.

"Why would she think Kala was the Priestess?" Seta looked at her. She decided to start over. Seta pointed to herself.

"Seta." Then she pointed to the other woman.

Tasira pointed to herself. "Tasira." And so, the conversation began.

Seta showed Tasira around the Temple of Kala. There were so many paintings on the walls for Tasira to see that soon, she became weary. Seta saw her new companion tiring and showed her to a lovely room with a flowing waterfall.

She showed Tasira the tiny room that had a pattern of holes in the ceiling. She pulled a lever and warm water spilled out and drained away through the floor. Seta pulled out some loose clothing and handed it to Tasira. Seta nodded and closed the door to the bedroom behind her.

Tasira took her clothes off and went into the shower. She used the wonderful smelling soap Seta had provided and dressed in the clean clothing she had been given. She looked around for her dirty clothing and her maps, but everything was gone. Someone had removed it while she was washing herself. All she had left was the robe-like garment Seta had left her.

"That was really stupid, Tasira. You can't leave now. Everything you own is gone." Tasira looked down in relief when she realized that she still had the medallion. She had left it on while she showered. At least there was that.

Chapter Twenty-One

Qata had been different since the meeting at the Hall of Elders. Nathaniel had tried to get her to go to the garden, go on picnics, or just to join him for the evening meal. She said no each time she was asked. She walked around, alone, during the middle of the night. Nathaniel could hear her footsteps outside his door, but she never knocked or came in to see him.

It had been too long and Nathaniel's patience had worn thin. He was going to confront her. Right now. It only took him a few moments to get to Qata's door. He turned the doorknob and walked in without knocking. Qata was startled and turned around. Nathaniel could see she had been crying.

"Why are you crying, Qata?" Nathaniel asked as he put his arms around her. She pulled away.

"There is nothing I could tell you to explain how I am feeling." Qata looked at him, "I want you to leave. I do not wish to bond with you any longer," she said cruelly as she pointed toward the door.

Nathaniel stepped back, but placed his hands on her arms. Qata winced. Nathaniel looked at her more closely and under the collar of her shirt he could see the shadow of bruising.

"Qata, you are coming with me whether you like it or not. We are going to see my father," he stated as he grabbed her wrist and drug her along the hallway. After the first few minutes, he realized that he would have to carry her. She was fighting every step of the way.

He threw Qata over his shoulder and carried her down to his father's study. Nathan could hear the screams, "No, I will not go!" coming closer. Nathan braced himself for the next onslaught. There wasn't much more that this family could take.

"Father, I brought Qata down to your study because she needs to tell you something!" Nathaniel said loudly, as he caught his breath. Qata went to the corner of the room and stood there with her arms crossed.

"Whatever it is that Qata needs to tell me, she needs to tell all of us in the Great Hall. You bring Qata, and I will get the others." That said, Nathan went to get his wife and children and told Caleb to get the others.

Once they were all assembled in the Great Hall, Nathan motioned for his son and Qata to stand at the head of the table. Qata stood stiffly, not saying a word. She glared at Nathaniel, but it didn't bother him in the least. They were finally going to get to the bottom of this odd behavior. Nathaniel took a deep breath and started the meeting.

"I am sure that many of you have wondered what has been happening between me and Qata." Nathaniel looked at Caleb, Ket, Jonathan, Pel and his parents. They all nodded.

"I needed to know, also, what was happening. So, I went to her room and opened the door without knocking. She was crying. I went to put her in my arms and she told me that she no longer wishes to bond with me," he looked over at Qata and she began crying again. Silent tears ran down her face as he spoke.

"Please Nathaniel, do not continue. You will spoil everything that I have tried to do." She looked over at him. "Please." She pleaded, "Don't."

"It will be alright, Qata. I promise you." Nathaniel looked at her for a moment and then held her hand. "When Qata told me she no longer wished to bond with me, I grabbed her arms. She winced as if she were in pain." He paused and looked at everyone at the table.

"I knew I had not grabbed her hard enough to hurt her." He paused. "Then I saw something under the collar of her shirt." Nathaniel looked at Mara.

"Mother, I need you to look at Qata. It would not be right for me to do this without being bonded to her." Mara nodded.

"Qata, I will need to look at your neck and arms. Please take off your sweater," she asked the young woman gently. When Qata finally complied, the whole room gasped. On her arms were black bruises the exact shape of a hand. It was also evident that someone scratched her until she bled. Mara continued to examine her. She opened the collar far enough to roll it down to her shoulders. Qata had multiple bruises on her neck and upper shoulders. Some of the bruising was fresh, other parts were showing signs of healing. It was obvious the young woman had been repeatedly hit and strangled by someone. Mara was pretty sure she knew that someone's name. Mara looked at Qata as she helped her button up her clothing.

"Did D'kal do this to you?" Qata looked up at Mara, but said nothing. Mara knew what it was like to be in Qata's place. Full of shame and guilt for not being able to stop what had happened.

"Qata, I want you to listen to me. I have a story to tell you," Qata nodded for Mara to continue.

Chapter Twenty-Two

"Back on my home world, Earth, I forced to serve in a terrible group called the Patrol. In the Patrol, there were men who had the power to do what they wanted." Mara looked at Qata. The young woman was looking at the floor. Mara grabbed Qata's chin, lightly, and made her look her in the eyes.

"After I left the Patrol, they captured me. I was young and had done something foolish. I left the people who loved me, thinking I could protect them." Mara cleared her throat at the uncomfortable memory.

"They threw me into the cells. Into a prison. It was a filthy place where a person could disappear and never be seen again." Mara squeezed Qata chin a little harder. "The men used me in any way they wanted. In ways I hope you can never imagine." Mara sighed.

"I was passed from man to man, not knowing if my death would come mercifully or if I would have to endure unending days of torture." Mara paused to gather her composure again.

"A young man, who was a soldier in the Patrol, helped me escape. At first, I didn't think it was true. I thought he would just shoot me. But I ran anyway. I was weak and humiliated and thought I didn't care if I lived or died. I was wrong. The men of this house came to save me, and Nathan loved me no matter what secrets I may have had. It did not matter to him." Mara looked over at her son and smiled.

"Nathaniel is very much his father's son. He will not care what has happened, only that you love him and that you are safe." She looked at Qata again.

"Now…tell him, and us, what has happened." Mara stood by her and nodded for her to tell everyone. It was a long pause before Qata began her story.

"As you know, I am not the daughter of D'kal. I am a half-breed. I am only half Kuutaran. I do not know the race of my father. My mother did not want me, so I was sold to the Kuutaran government." Qata swallowed hard, and looked nervously at the faces fixed on her.

"I was very young when the government decided that I was old enough to work in one of the houses to earn my keep. It was the same house D'kal worked in and she took great delight in making me do things for the men who paid her." Qata bit at her lip.

"When D'kal got Tavon to marry her, she asked him to buy my debt to the government. He did and I was to act as if D'kal was my mother. I believe that she told Tavon that I was her daughter....at first." She looked down at the table and then back up. Her eyes flashed in defiance.

"She is evil. She has no problem killing, lying, cheating, or anything else she needs to do to attain her goals." Qata closed her eyes and took a deep breath. She stopped speaking and after a long wait, Mara spoke to her.

"Qata, you must finish your story. It is the only way we can help you," Mara looked at her in empathy. "I know that this is difficult but you must finish."

"I don't want to tell you what I have done," she said quietly, "I would rather leave here with my secrets and return to D'kal, than to have you look at me with hate."

"I do not care what it is, we will resolve it together." Nathaniel smiled softly. Qata looked at him and tears fell down her face. She nodded and continued.

"I had known Nathaniel for a month and wanted to be with him, but I knew that it was something that would never come to pass. It seemed to be a miracle when D'kal told me I was going to live at the House of Nathan. But I knew that there was a motive behind her change of heart." Qata looked around at the others.

"I was to come here so that D'kal could falsely accuse you of holding me against my will." She pressed her lips together. "The other part of the agreement was that I was to find Mara's medallion and steal it. She wanted the power and status it would bring her." Qata raised her head and smiled a bit.

"I was to report to her twice a week. Each time she was angry because I had failed." Qata removed her sweater, and her shirt, standing in front of the others in only an undergarment. "This is what she did when I told her that the medallion was gone and lost forever."

The amount of bruising that they had been unable to see was staggering. Qata had bruises all over her body. The scars that were not visible before had the unique pattern of Kuutaran fingernail strikes. It was beyond appalling. No one spoke for a while. The Great Hall remained silent until Nathan stood up and looked at Qata.

"I need to have the Elders look at these bruises without D'kal knowing about it. They need to know of her crimes." Nathan looked at Qata again. "Are you up to the challenge?" Qata nodded her head and smiled. It was the first time anyone had ever seen her smile that widely. She looked free. Nathan nodded to Tamara to come over by him. He whispered something in her ear. She looked up at him with twinkling eyes. His eldest daughter was definitely game for this gambit. It would take some time, but it would be worth the wait.

Chapter Twenty-Three

It had been a couple of weeks since Aziz had brought the strange woman into Mabray. It had taken quite a while for her to be able to walk out in the sun again. He saw her ze'ev, Tinku, run ahead of her and sniff the wind.

"Tinku!" Aziz called playfully at the animal. "Come here!" Tinku ran over to him and licked his arm. It was like having a sticky mud on his arm. Not exactly what he intended, but the result was perfect. Tasira was walking his way. Perhaps she would ask him to walk with her again. He could not wait until she could speak the same language as he did. But they seemed to get along alright without words. Tinku ran back to his mistress, tail wagging. Tasira shook her head and laughed at the animal.

"You would run off with anyone that would give you a scratch on the top of your head, wouldn't you?"

She laughed again. Tasira looked at the large male that was further down the walkway and waved. She had learned that his name was Aziz. It took a while to master his name in the old dialect, but now she could also say thank you to him when he walked with her. Tasira walked the sort distance to Aziz and smiled.

"Hello, Aziz." She motioned to the walkway. "Will you walk with me?"

"Y'en," Aziz answered and nodded. He couldn't help himself. He was smiling like the village idiot, but it didn't matter to him. He was walking with the beautiful and kind woman again tonight. Tasira. Even her name was beautiful.

"I wish I could really talk with you, Aziz." She looked up at his face and smiled. "I wish I could learn the language faster. But there is no way to do that, is there?" Aziz looked down at her and smiled again.

"I wish there was some way I could talk to Tasira." Aziz thought as he looked down at her. *"But there is no way to make things go any faster."* The smile slowly left his face. *"It is probably for the best anyway. We will have nothing in common after she learns our language. The walks will be done and she will find her perfect mate in another male's arms.*

Tasira saw the change come over his face. It was now stoic and devoid of emotion. She reached for his hand and placed hers inside. Her hand had completely disappeared and she giggled a bit. This drew his attention back down to her. He looked at her smiling face and took her laughter as something completely different.

"Even she finds me too different." Aziz tried to take his hand away but Tasira held on tightly. Aziz looked down again and could not disguise the sorrow on his face.

Why is he so sad? What has changed in the last few minutes?" Tasira looked at him, confused. She pulled him to a stop.

"What is going on with you tonight," she asked him, knowing he wouldn't understand her. Then, the answer hit her. He thought she had laughed at *him*! She would settle this right now!

"Aziz?" She asked him quietly. Aziz nodded. "I know you cannot understand me, but I was not laughing at you." Aziz looked at her quizzically. Tasira looked up at him pointedly and then grabbed his hand and kissed the rough skin of his palm. Aziz was astounded.

"I must say thank you for the walk," Tasira looked up at him. "*Gaaday 'nu.*" She put her hand on her heart.

"I will see you tomorrow." She finished as she pulled her hand from his and finished the short walk to her new home. She left Aziz standing, with his eyes wide, as he watched her walk away.

"She kissed my hand and then walked away. What does that mean?" Aziz asked himself. He shook his head at his foolishness. He walked away and continued until he reached the small home that was now his. He started mumbling to himself.

"She has no idea what I am. How can I let her think that I am like the rest of the men here?" Aziz swiped a hand over his bald head as he looked in the mirror before him. He saw how large he was and threw a pottery cup across the room. It shattered into a perfect circle of dust and shards on the floor.

"I am Xoran. Perhaps she does not know what that means." He paced across the floor and looked at himself once again. His dark tanned skin was leathery-smooth like Tasira's messenger bag. His eyes were as blue as the sky of his home world, and he had very little hair on his body. He did have some Tuulan features. The shape of his face was a mixture of his mother's Tuulan ancestry and his father's Xoran warrior appearance. He was imposing, to say the least.

He thought about Tasira. She had fine golden hair covering her body, but not as thick as the others, and long black hair on top of her head. She looked every bit a Tuulan except for her size.

Her eyes were the deepest green he had ever seen. Perhaps that was part of her other ancestry too. He had never seen a Tuulan with eyes that color. He wished he could ask her these things, but he would never have the chance. Those questions were asked after you are bonded, and he would never be bonding with her. This much he was sure of. He had vowed, long ago, to never try to bond with a female again. But time had a way of giving opportunity where none appeared to exist.

Chapter Twenty-Four

A year had passed and Tasira had become fluent in the old dialect. Aziz and many of the others were learning her language in return, making it easier to freely converse with the people of Mabray. Mabray, was apparently the ancient word for 'of the desert'.

Tasira had learned many things since she had arrived. She was, in return, able to tell them of the city she came from and the world she was born on. It was a long night, every story night, for the following week.

Every night, afterward, she asked Aziz to come with her on her walk and he would smile and nod his head. She realized, after the first few evenings that Aziz was the large shadowy figure that had carried her out of the sands and into Mabray. She knew now why she had gotten so much shade.

Aziz was a large, formidable looking male. Tasira was also pretty sure that he was not as fierce inside as he looked on the outside.

During the first few nights she told them of her quest across the sand. They explained that they had found her when Tinku came to them and led them back to her. The poor animal had run the entire way to Mabray and back to her. He collapsed from dehydration once they had reached her.

They put the animal on a stretcher, Tasira in one of the men's arms, and carried them both back to the town. Tinku jumped into the bottom of the spring where it pooled and returned to the ground. He drank water until he could barely move, which was when they were able to finally wash him. He was a new animal when he laid down next to Tasira. He laid there until she awakened two days later.

Tonight, Tasira was going to show everyone the documents she had brought with her. She pinned the map of the city to the wall with some sap from the tree. She did the same with the other documents. She was nervous about showing them the document that ordered the death of any child that was deemed substandard. But unfortunately, sometimes the truth was ugly.

"Hello Tasira!" Seta spoke in a happy voice. "What wonders are you going to show us this evening?"

"What I have tonight may be something that you will not want to hear. It may make you angry." Tasira looked at Seta with serious sorrow in her eyes. Seta could feel the grief and fear that her friend was feeling. It was her gift and curse.

Experiencing other's emotions could be an exhausting experience. Seta had learned long ago how to block these emotions from invading her mind. Since Tasira arrived, Seta had let her guard down to better understand the young female who had travelled the blistering sands to reach them.

She knew that Tasira had no intentions of harming anyone, but tonight her friend was carrying a deep burden and the grief was almost too much to bear. It felt too heavy in her chest, she decided to go to her room and focus on not letting any more into her mind than the actual story tonight.

After preparing everything, Tasira went out for a walk to clear her mind and enjoy the cooling breeze that was coming with the setting of the suns. Mabray was such a pretty place. That it survived in the middle of nowhere made it even more amazing.

The trees in the village provided unending fruits. And other plants grew on one side of the flowing water. A small barn had been built on the edge of the village where they raised ezza'a. The ezza'a had silky hair which was used for spinning cloth. When the animal became old, they were slaughtered for food. There was nothing in this place that was taken for granted or wasted.

As Tasira walked around, Aziz watched her from the shadows. She looked sad tonight and he wondered why. But he would not go and speak with her. He didn't want to get comfortable with the idea of being close with her. He watched as Tinku ran up to her with his tail wagging. A few minutes later someone else joined her on her walk.

"Tasira, do you need some help setting up the Great Hall for tonight's story?" Gan asked with a smile. There was a step up and Gan held out his hand to assist Tasira. Tasira smiled, accepted the noble gesture, and then shook her head.

"I have everything set up. I just thought I would enjoy some fresh air before everyone showed up." Tasira looked up at Gan and smiled.

"There is much I have to tell tonight and some will be unpleasant. It may even anger some of you." Tasira stopped walking and grabbed Gan's hand.

"I appreciate your company, but tonight I would like to be alone for a little while." She dropped his hand and continued walking. Gan watched her walk off and smiled a little.

Aziz realized he had placed dents in the tree he stood under. Then it dawned on him that he had gotten angry when Tasira had walked with Gan. He shook his head and walked away from his hidden spot. He would not spy on her again. It would only end up with him being miserable. His heart couldn't take any more of his daydreams. A Xoran male could never be with a woman like Tasira. Aziz walked around the shadowed edges of the village until it was time for tonight's story.

Chapter Twenty-Five

Tasira watched as all of the town ambled into the large Great Hall. There was laughing and smiling and a festive attitude as they walked in but Tasira felt none of this. She was scared of what was going to happen if they decided to throw her out of the city with nothing but her documents and Tinku. She would not make it back to the city without the help of the residents of Mabray.

Tasira saw the large man who had once caught her as she fell from a tree. Aziz had been catching her attention ever since. She enjoyed his company on her walks even though the conversation was sporadic at best.

As usual, he smiled at her, blushed a little as he avoided her gaze and sat in the back of the room. He never sat up front. One night, she asked him why and he told her he sat in the back because he was too big. He wanted the others behind him to be able to see. So, he, respectfully sat in the back.

Tasira walked to where Aziz sat. As she got closer, he became more uncomfortable. She smiled at him sweetly and watched as the large man looked at her hopefully. All the thoughts he had earlier in the evening melted away and all he could do was think of how much he wanted to be with her. Just to be next to her would be enough for him.

Tasira sat down next to him, "I want to talk to you for a moment, if you don't mind."

"Mind?" Aziz thought to himself as he shook his head no. "No, I do not mind," he stammered. He felt like kicking himself. He sounded so stupid. "What would you like to tell me, Tasira?"

"It's about the things I will tell everyone tonight," she whispered. "It is not happy information. It may make you hate me." Tasira paused for a moment.

"Before that happens, I want to tell you that I think you are a wonderful man," she bent over and kissed him on the cheek and then whispered into his ear. "I wish things were different. I wish I could be with you, forever." She looked at the surprised stares they were getting. Every person in the room stopped talking.

"I am sorry to embarrass you." Tasira quickly moved toward the front of the room.

Aziz was completely dumbfounded. He couldn't think of a single thing to say. He was always the one she asked when she wanted to take Tinku for a walk, but he thought that she chose him because he was the biggest man. You know, to protect her.

They always had nice conversations and she was always kind to him. He never had that type of kindness before. He was respected for being Xoran, but kindness from others, especially a female, was not usual for him. Xoran males were extremely large and fierce, but that was not the part of him that he felt inside. He did not want to harm anyone and doubted that there would be anything that could bring that merciless part of him to the forefront.

Unless someone wanted to hurt Tasira or, apparently, if they wanted to take her away. That became quite clear this evening. Beautiful and kind Tasira. He nodded slightly at that thought. She might be the only reason he would hurt someone. Tasira took her place at the front of the room and Aziz found himself watching her every move.

"Tonight, I have to tell you some things that may surprise you. And, possibly anger you." Tasira looked around the room at all of the kind faces that had taken her in and saved her life.

"You may want to cast me out of your city when I am done. If that is the case, it will be a small price to pay for the truth." Tasira took a deep breath and began the story of the reason there were so few Tuulans left on Tuulani. Within an hour, she was finished.

"The proclamation from the Elders happened a long time in the past. But I believe that this place was built to save the children. I think that somehow this place was their destination, but do not know how."

"Well, then let me tell you a story," said Seta. "This story happened a long time ago as well," she smiled at Tasira. Tasira was confused. Why weren't they angry? Seta began her story.

"Many hundreds of years ago, there was a gleaming city. It was the jewel of Tuulani, its name has been lost over the generations, but it was named for the first Priestess. The Priestess kept Tuulani safe and prosperous, but the men desired to have control of the city. They devised a plan to rid themselves of the Priestess, and destroy her control of Tuulani." Seta looked at everyone in the room. She had never told the whole story to her people before. They were hanging on Seta's every word.

"The Priestess discovered the plan and put obstacles in their path, so that they could not reach her. She would make the winds blow and the rains flood the city, but they were not to be denied. They threw a poison in the Priestess's spring. She drew the water from the spring and drank from her cup. After the first drink, she knew she was going to die. She could feel the poison racing through her organs." Seta paused for effect.

"She put the essence of her knowledge into a sacred library so that she could find the next Priestess and all of her successors. They say that the city can see her when they need her wisdom, but her full knowledge is locked up until she finds the right female to be the next Priestess." Seta smiled at Tasira, "You see, there are stories here too, that you do not tell your children until they are older."

"You say she became part of the city?" Tasira asked tentatively.

"Yes, the Priestess does not reveal her true nature until she finds the next female who is worthy of her full knowledge. She will remain in the library and will only reveal herself fully, when she finds the next potential Priestess." Seta paused and looked hard at Tasira. "Why do you ask? It is only a story. Actually, more of a fable. The Priestess is not real."

Tasira looked at Seta seriously, not knowing whether or not to tell her more. She looked at Aziz and knew that she had to tell everyone the truth.

"I have seen the visage of the Priestess. I can assure you she is real." Tasira looked around.

"She is the one who showed me the map. She gave me the other knowledge I possess. Her name is Batah." A silence fell over the group and then suddenly everyone started talking at the same time. Seta calmed the group and then turned her attention back to Tasira.

"You are sure that you saw the Priestess?" she asked, not knowing whether to believe Tasira or not.

"How many times did you see her? Were there others that saw her too? How did she appear to you? " Seta fired questions one after the other. Tasira held up one hand.

"I did not know she was the Priestess. Not until you told me of her legend." Tasira looked up at Seta.

"I do not think that anyone knows that Batah is the visage of the Priestess. I have heard of other females becoming a Priestess, but they did not have the power of the one you speak about. There has been no Priestess for three hundred years."

"This is the woman who helped you after you found the hidden staircase?" Seta looked hard at Tasira. Tasira nodded.

"She showed you the library?" Seta inquired. Again, Tasira nodded. Seta motioned to Tasira.

"Then I must show you this," Seta said as she grabbed Tasira's hand and led her to another room. The others followed the young women to see this new room for themselves. It was behind a hidden door that Seta opened as she walked through it. She lit a lamp and the room revealed its contents. It was a library like the one Tasira found in the old wing of her home.

Chapter Twenty-Six

"We have not been able to understand how this room works. But I have been told that it is a library that hold the secrets of our beginning." Seta said in a melancholy voice.

"Do you understand this room and how it functions?" Seta asked. Tasira nodded as she picked up a jewel from the ornate box.

"These are the books," Tasira picked up a jewel, "and that space holds the jewel." She placed the jewel into the correct position and it began to glow.

"When you place your hand over the jewel, it shows you, in your mind, the knowledge that it holds. Would you like to go first Seta?" Seta shook her head.

"You go first, and tell me what you see," she said to Tasira in a wavering voice. Tasira understood the fear of the unknown. It was that way when Batah first showed her the library, too. Tasira nodded.

"Alright Seta, I will go first. But you must understand that I will not be able to tell you about the book until it is finished. The speed that the information enters my thoughts is too quick for me to keep up with speech. Do you understand what I mean?" Seta nodded and motioned for Tasira to show her how it worked.

Tasira walked over to the console that held the glowing gem. She placed her hand over the jewel and a flood of images went through her mind.

She could see a young couple and their baby. They were being banished into the Outlands to die. They had refused to give their baby up to be murdered. She was born with a foot that was turned in and shriveled. She was never going to be able to walk normally. The male took out six strange metal objects out of the baby's blanket. The first two were placed in the sand where the infants were left to die. The last four were nataks, doorways to another place. One was buried just outside the wall, two more were placed between two large rocks and the last one they took with them when they opened a doorway to this place. Mabray.

They built a home with bricks made from the sticky mud by the end of the stream. When the natak glowed, they would return to the spot outside the city and retrieve the infants that were abandoned. They would feed the infant a liquid that would neutralize the poison it had been given.

Each child would be healed by a woman's medallion that the female brought with her. Each time she used it she became weak, but she wanted the children to live full lives. The names of the two parents were Dorn and Gayla. They saved over a hundred infants before they died of old age. The images stopped and Tasira sat down to catch her breath as she always did when she viewed a book.

Tasira told the story of the book to Seta and the others. They were astonished. They had a box containing an old artifact. No one knew what it was, but the box had the names Dorn and Gayla carved into it. It also had held a medallion that had been passed down to the eldest female of the family. Seta was the one who wore it now.

"May I look at the box and its contents?" asked Tasira. Seta nodded and asked one of the others that was standing behind Tasira to get the old box. When Tul returned, he handed the box to Tasira.

As she opened top, she could see the same beautiful, iridescent black metal her mother wore around her finger. The ring her father, Nathan, had given to her mother Mara. It seemed to swirl around without moving. When Tasira put the object in her hand the red gem in the center started to glow. Everyone drew in a deep breath as the red gem pulsed red light. Tasira turned around to face the crowd.

"This is the natak that Dorn and Gayla used to arrive here. It allowed them to retrieve the infants that were abandoned. You are the lost children of the city." A realization hit her. These people hadn't been genetically changed by their ancestors. The people of Mabray were almost pure Tuulan. They were perfectly imperfect. She put a hand over her mouth to quell the emotions this brought forth.

"You are the secret to keeping Tuulani alive." Tasira spoke in broken sentences as she turned around to look at the entire group.

"You are the past and the future all in one." Tasira's eyes opened wider at her next thought. "This is why Batah sent me to find you. She knew I would bring you back if you wanted to return with me." She looked at all of them.

"You are the lost children of Tuulani," she repeated in a soft voice filled with awe.

That statement was met with loud voices speaking all at once. "We are not lost. We should not go…I do not believe her...I wonder what the city looks like..." and on it went until Aziz went and stood by Tasira.

"I believe her. She would not come here to tell you a lie. Do you not remember that she almost died out in the sands? You may ask her questions, but you will be respectful to her." Aziz finished in a low rumbling voice. The escalating mob mentality died out as quickly as it had started.

Aziz nodded at Tasira and gently touched her hand with his. He looked away after he did so, embarrassed that he had touched her at all. Tasira looked up at him and grabbed his hand and held it tight. She smiled at him and everything in the room seemed to disappear but her. He found himself smiling when the other voices reappeared and the moment was lost.

Seta saw the exchange between the two of them and smiled a little to herself. Of all the males in the village, Aziz would have been the last one she would've thought to pair up with Tasira. The mismatch in size, itself, was beyond explanation. By the way other males had looked at her, she could have chosen anyone. But Seta was happy for the both of them. She knew that Aziz had given up on ever completing the bonding ceremony. The way Tasira looked at him, though, it wouldn't take too long for the two of them to figure it out

Tasira had come to the library with Seta every day for the last two months. They both had viewed the books and were now finishing the last few left in the library. They had discovered the way to hunt for food and the proper way to filter the water so they would not get ill, and many other tidbits of wisdom. The practical knowledge itself was worth more than anyone could have expected.

These were the things that her father would need to know to help the city become self-sufficient again. She longed to see her family again, but she knew that she must wait for the sign the last book she viewed at *her* library had shown her.

Seta and Tasira finished the last book at Mabray and started to leave the room. One of the Elders, Lyn, walked up to them. He had a serious look on his face. Tasira and Seta smiled at the old male and greeted him.

"What brings you here, Lyn," asked Seta. The old male looked nervous as his gaze moved over to Tasira.

"You say that you are from the city, correct?" He watched her face carefully as he spoke to her.

Tasira looked at him oddly. She had told everyone where she was from the night she awakened here. "Yes, I am from the city across the sands." Lyn looked at her again and then nodded his head and walked away. Tasira looked at Seta.

"What was that all about?" she asked in confusion.

"I have no idea, but Lyn never does anything without a specific reason. He will tell you when the time is right." Seta looked at the old male as he walked away, wondering too what this question was all about.

Chapter Twenty-Seven

"It has been too long, Tavon!" D'kal was yelling at her husband again. He was glad that he had the means to keep his liquor flowing freely. It did help to some degree.

"My dear, dear wife. The Elders will call us when they want to talk to us again," he slurred. "You cannot rush the Elders into anything. They work on their own sense of time." This further incensed D'kal.

"Do you want to be Ra Shan of the city?" D'kal asked in a harsh tone.

"Of course, D'kal. I want to be Ra Shan so that you can manipulate the entire city with the strings you have attached to me like a child's puppet." Tavon smiled at D'kal while he was wobbling around in his chair. "You will get exactly what you deserve my dear. But the Elders will not be rushed."

"What of your son, Foro. Don't you want him to have a place of importance in the city?" She badgered him again. Tavon smiled.

"My son," he paused, "My son?" Tavon frowned a little. "You and I both know that the little bastard isn't mine. It was just convenient that you became pregnant when we met." He looked at D'kal and smiled.

"If anyone were to look in the book of Elders, they would read about a child being born. His name was Tavon, and he would not have the ability to create a child in a woman's womb. He was born with a medical condition and was unable to make a child." Tavon looked at D'kal who was now infuriated.

"You see, my love, I have no children unless I agree to take them as mine officially. You and your bastard son would be thrown out of this house and there would be nothing left for you to steal if I decided to rescind my declaration. The one that makes Foro my son." He paused and smiled.

"I let you believe that you have the power." Tavon smiled a bit as he took another sip from his glass. "But the power was never in your possession." He stared into his glass.

"I already gave a letter to the attendant at the Hall of Elders. It will be opened in the event of my death." Tavon smiled.

"You are as helpless as a babe, and at my mercy. Once they see your deceit, you will be sent back to Kuutarii. You had best hope, D'kal, that your mate has a long life." Tavon pushed himself up again in his chair. D'kal narrowed her eyes in fury.

"Do you remember the day we went to the Elders to ask if Foro could become an attendant? You were so furious that Nathan's daughter had been asked. You realize it was because she had told the truth and had shown the Elders the type of boy Foro was. They could see it." Tavon continued sternly.

"They told you as much when you begged them to reconsider. You want to remove those men who judged you and Foro. To me it makes no difference, I have no vested interest in your boy. I only protect you two from a worse fate because it suits me to do so. I have a du'lupa of my very own," he smiled.

"I no longer have to pay for the services you provide. The whore gives me what I want, freely, in return for my favor." Tavon finished his drink and walked unsteadily towards his room. D'kal growled and raged at Tavon as he walked away. She threw glasses and anything else she could reach. He just continued to walk until he reached his room and closed the door. After Tavon was out of sight, D'kal sat down and thought about the next best course of action.

Shortly after Qata had told the truth about her betrayal and her reasons, Tamara went out the door to the Hall of Elders. She pretended to ask about her training to be an attendant and went inside the foyer to wait. She used the ruse to misdirect the spies she knew D'kal had in the city.

D'kal paid credits out generously when there was news about the House of Nathan. Tammy had learned about this when her best friend Wynn whispered to Tammy about not speaking too much about her family. Tammy had asked why and Wynn told her that her parents had been offered credits. A whole year's worth if the information panned out.

Wynn's parents had refused the offer and D'kal accused them of stealing from her home. The Elders had called for Batah to confirm whether or not Wynn's parents had ever been to the House of Tavon. Batah looked as far back as when her parents were children. She made it clear that neither of Wynn's parents had ever been in, or around, the House of Tavon. D'kal was told to search her house once more and if the item was still missing, she should come back and report it. D'kal never returned.

As Tamara waited, she noticed the young male who was the attendant today. He was very handsome and Tamara was not shy.

"May I ask your name?" she asked outright. The young male looked back at her and smiled.

"My name is Ket." he stated simply. Tamara blinked a couple of times as she stared at him. "What is wrong?" the young male asked with concern.

"Nothing," she said softly. "That is my great-grandfather's name. I have never heard of anyone else having his name. He was very important when we were on Earth. It was because of him that my father is still alive. He kept the entire village safe when he was the Elder."

"You had Elders on your home world too?" Ket asked in astonishment. "How did they keep the bloodline going?" he asked.

"The males would go and find a human female to bond with, but when the time came to give birth, most of the females could not survive." Tamara continued, "Every female that had given birth, except for my mother, died during childbirth. The females born in our house were the first that had ever been seen by the village. All of the other babes were male and grew up without ever knowing their mothers."

Tamara looked at him with a sadness far beyond her years. As she finished the last sentence, one of the large doors opened and Jes looked out at Ket and cleared his throat. The young male was embarrassed and ran over to the door.

"The Elders will speak with you now," he spoke with a blush to his cheeks.

Tamara walked into the large Hall of Elders and heard the door close behind her. She looked up the Elders and nodded to each of them. Jes just couldn't stay mad at this annoyingly charming young female. She had a way about her that combined trustworthiness, seriousness in her honesty and impish fun all in one mind. He could hardly wait to see the type of woman she would develop into.

"I understand that you are asking about becoming an attendant. I thought we had decided that you would have to mature a bit before we would accept your request." Jes looked at her with a slight frown.

"Yes, you are correct. But I have mislead you about the reason I am really here," Tamara looked directly at each of the Elders.

"I am sorry to have resort to these tactics, but it was the only way I could come here without the House of Tavon hearing the real reason. D'kal has offered credits to anyone who will deliver information about my family." Jes's back straightened and he glared at Tamara.

"How do you know this is true?" he asked Tammy sharply. This was a serious accusation.

"My best friend is Wynn. Her parents Tal and U'na, were asked to get information about our family. They refused. They are honorable and have been good friends to our family." Tamara paused a moment.

"As you know, Wynn's parents they were charged with stealing something from D'kal. She had hoped to scare them into giving her information, but she failed. I fear that now, as the decision to choose a Ra Shan grows nearer, D'kal will become more forceful in her tactics." Tammy looked directly at Jes and straightened her posture. "But that is not the reason I am here today."

Jes looked at her and then the other eight member that formed the Council of Elders. They looked at the young female standing in front of them. Each of them nodded their approval to Jes. They could feel the gravity of Tamara's words and knew it must be serious.

"Why then, Tammy, do you seek our counsel. Has someone done something to your family?" Tamara nodded. Jes motioned to her, "Then please continue." Tamara took a deep breath.

"You know that Qata has been living in our household for many months. We have been accused of holding her against her will, but that is not true." Tammy looked at the floor to tamp down the anger she was feeling. After another deep breath, she continued.

"Nathaniel and Qata were seeing each other in secret for a long time before she ever entered our home. Apparently D'kal had heard of this and decided to use Qata to get what she wanted." Tammy looked back at the council members with the anger she could no longer hide.

"Information and revenge." She finished. Jes held up his hand to stop Tamara.

"Revenge for what?" he asked. The anger left Tammy's face and was replaced with shame as she hung her head.

"It was all my fault. Tasira had always been different from the other children at school. She was always quiet and shy and couldn't adjust to being away from Mother all day. This made her the favorite target for mean words. But Foro, and the others, were starting to find more than words to hurt Tasira." A tear fell down Tammy's cheek as she thought about the sister she would never see again in this life.

"The last day Tasira went to school, Foro encouraged some of the others to begin throwing stones and other things at my sister. When Foro threw his metal toy soldier, it hit Tasira and gouged her arm." Tammy looked at Jes, "I went over and hit Foro in the eye and told everyone there that the next person who hurt my family would get the same." She sighed, "I am not proud of what I did that day. I wish I could take it all back because now D'kal seeks revenge." Jes nodded at her.

"Alright, I understand that part now, but why do you need our help today?" Jes asked.

"My father wants you to see what D'kal has done to Qata. It is awful. I do not know how many beatings she has endured." Jes stopped her again.

"Why would she hurt her?" Jes asked, puzzled.

"Qata is not her daughter. She was sold to the Kuutaran Government when her mother abandoned her. She was working in the same, um, house as D'kal." Tamara stumbled over the words, not knowing how to say such things.

"In the same house as D'kal? But we were told that D'kal had come from a family of the ruling class on

Kuutarii. Is this not true?" Jes asked. Tammy's face turned red.

"I do not know how to say these things. It makes me embarrassed." Tammy turned away. Jes got up from his seat and walked over to where Tammy stood.

"You may whisper it in my ear and I will tell the others for you. Would that be easier?" Tammy nodded at Jes and leaned over to whisper in his ear. As she whispered, Jes's eyebrow shot up almost to the top of his forehead.

"It's alright Tammy, I will tell them." Eight sets of eyes were fixed on Jes.

"D'kal and the young Qata were working in a house where they were paid to have relations with various men. D'kal worked there as a means to find a powerful husband. Qata was forced to work there to pay the government for the expense of raising her. D'kal bought Qata's debt when she left and married Tavon. She introduced her as her daughter, but she is really D'kal's slave." The outraged gasp from the Elders echoed inside the Hall.

"So, it is true," one of the Elders spoke. The Council of Nine had been deliberating on what D'kal's true relationship had been with Qata. It was now clear. Jes looked at Tamara.

"Am I understanding this correctly? You want us to see the young female without having to bring her to us. Is this correct?" Tammy nodded at the old Tuulan.

"It is the only way we can prove our allegations and still keep Qata safe. My father is sure D'kal would find a way to kill her if she knew that Qata had told us everything." Tamara pleaded. "Please help us, we do not want Qata to be hurt again."

"Alright Tamara," Jes said, "Let's go speak with your parents."

"Wait!" Tamara spoke up, "If anyone sees you, D'kal will know what Qata has told us."

Jes smiled and went over to the ornate case on the altar. He opened it and took out a map of the city. He motioned for Tamara to come over and take a look.

"Do you see the Hall of Elders in the center of the city?" Jes pointed. Tamara nodded. "And do you see these five dark dotted lines. Each one leading to the major houses in the city?" Again, Tamara nodded.

"These, my dear young lady, are tunnels from the Hall of Elders to those houses. It is a secret long held from anyone but the Elders. Today, I think it is time to use the tunnel to your house to our advantage." Jes winked at Tamara and she smiled broadly and hugged the old Tuulan. Jes was surprised at the impulsive act, but he could tell she didn't do such things very often.

Jes grabbed a small stack of Hermes paper, and packed it in a carrying case hidden behind the statue of the Priestess. He told Tammy to go out the same door she had come in. Doing so would diminish the curiosity of anyone watching. After she left and closed the large doors, all nine Elders went to the House of Nathan in secret.

Chapter Twenty-Eight

The sun was setting on the horizon and Nathan and Mara were worried about their eldest daughter. Seconds later Tamara came in the front door. She looked calm, as if nothing happened. But as soon as she closed the door her countenance changed from calm to excited.

"They are coming here?" Mara whispered. Her eyes opened wider, "Everyone will see them!"

"No one will see them, Mother. They have a way to arrive here without anyone knowing. Trust me." Tamara smiled at her mother.

"How will they get here without anyone seeing them?" Nathan asked her. Tamara shook her head.

"I cannot tell you. It is a secret held by the Elders. I am not able to share the knowledge with anyone else. I cannot betray their confidence." Tammy folded both arms across her chest and looked at her parents. It was evident that she wouldn't tell anyone.

"Good girl, Tamara. I knew our secrets would be safe with you!" Jes said as he walked down the staircase to the foyer. "Now where is Qata so that we can speak to all of you together?"

"I will go and get everyone assembled in the Great Hall." Tamara nodded respectfully to the nine Elders. They nodded back and looked at Mara.

"You have a fine daughter, Mara." Jes smiled. "I suspect that she is much like her mother." Mara blushed and thanked Jes for his kindness. Mara realized, belatedly, the Elders were standing out in the foyer and she had not invited them into the Great Hall to sit down. She offered them a seat and then went to help Caleb make something to offer their guests. Mara sent Tammy to tell the others to come to the Great Hall for the meeting. She watched Tammy as she walked away. Her eldest girl was a young woman to be proud of.

The entire House of Nathan was quickly gathered in the Great Hall, including Qata. They all sat in quiet, a little uneasy that the Elders had somehow appeared in their home. Jes looked at Tamara and nodded.

"Qata," Tammy said softly, "The Elders are here because my father asked me to speak to them about your difficulties. They know everything that you told us and they are here to document your statement, and your injuries, for the official record." She went over to the Kuutaran girl and grabbed her hand.

"I know this must be overwhelming, but you must tell them everything. They will find a way to help you." Tammy led Qata over to the Elders. Nathaniel joined them as the three stood in front of the Council of Nine.

Qata told the entire story to the Elders and everyone else at the table as well. Nathaniel was outraged. There were some things that D'kal made her do that were beyond cruel. The young woman cried as she told the entire tale. When she had finished, Jes motioned for Tamara to come closer.

"Since Tamara was the one to tell us first, and since she is another female who can protect Qata's honor, we will all adjourn to a private room. There we can see the injuries on Qata' body." Nathaniel started to say something, but Jes held up his hand and pointed at him.

"Do not ask young man! You are not this girl's mate, yet, and you cannot come into the room with us. That decision is final!" Jes looked at Nathaniel sternly. As they walked to the first private room, Qata grabbed Tamara's hand and whispered, "Thank You." Tammy smiled at her and they entered the room together.

Tamara help Qata undress behind the screen. She was appalled at the scarring and bruising she had under her shirt and pants. She helped Qata remove all of her clothing except for her bottom undergarments. Tamara took a long piece of cloth from the closet behind her and placed it over Qata's breasts and tied it behind her. Then she gave her a long robe to cover up as she walked out in front of the Elders.

It took a couple of hours for the Elders to ask her questions and document her injuries. The collective gasp from the men when she showed them her neck was deafening in the quiet room. As Qata showed other injuries, Tamara made sure that the other parts of the girl's body were not exposed. Finally, the examination was over and Qata returned to the screen and dressed once again.

With the notes taken and the record completed, the Elders went back to the Great Hall. All eyes were upon them as they sat down and the anticipation of their ruling was immense. It was Pel who started the conversation.

"My name is Pel and I was the doctor on Earth when we lived there. How severe are the injuries," he inquired. Jes looked at Pel and then looked down.

"The injuries themselves are severe enough, but the damage done to her mind is more severe. She has endured more humiliation than anyone can imagine. Some of this was due to the so-called 'debt' she owed the government, but the majority of it was due to D'kal. From what I can gather, D'kal has never been a mother or friend to Qata." Jes looked directly at Nathaniel.

"Whoever bonds with this female will have to be gentle, firm, and understanding. Qata has never had a normal relationship in her life. Perhaps the bonding will fill these deficits. But more than likely, she will have difficulty accepting that she is safe and in a loving relationship. The bonding could be difficult." Jes finished. Mara stood up and looked at Jes.

"I do not wish to argue with you, but Qata has had almost the same life I had before I met Nathan. " She looked over and smiled at her mate.

"We had our difficulties, but we have worked through the bad times together. I think you might be misjudging Qata. She is strong and I think she will work through her nightmares, too." Mara finished, looking at all of the men seated along the table. Jes paused, considering Mara's words.

"Perhaps Mara know best in this matter. She has survived the nightmares only a female could endure.

Perhaps Qata will be alright if she is given the support she needs." He looked at Nathan.

"There is still the matter of D'kal's crimes and the tenuous situation we are facing. We will not say anything to Tavon or D'kal. But Qata will no longer go to meet D'kal to give her information." Jes paused, "We will see what rodents her absence will flush out of the shadows." A smirk touched the corner of Jes's mouth as he led the Elders up the stairs again. Within a minute, the sound of their footsteps disappeared.

Chapter Twenty-Nine

Tasira was looking out across the swirling sands that were just beyond this paradise. How did Mabray survive out here all of these years and no one notice? It made her sad to think that these people were the descendants of the throw away children. These people would not have been born if it weren't for one brave couple. The babes they had saved were the great-grandparents of the citizens now living here. Now they were a self-sufficient village. There was something special about them, something unique.

And then there was Aziz. Handsome, kind Aziz. Tasira knew what the other women had told her about the Xorans, but she didn't think that those ruthless warrior qualities were inside his heart. He was shy and quiet. He walked with her every night. He made her feel like the princess she had once pretended to be. She had fallen in love with the man and she would find a way to show him that what she had told him was true. She wanted to be with him forever.

"Tasira?" came a familiar low voice. "May I sit by you?" Aziz asked.

"Of course, you can." Tasira smiled. "I was just looking out into the sea of sand. It seems to go on forever, but I know there is something out there." She glanced sideways at Aziz. "Have you ever been anywhere else than here?" Aziz nodded. Tasira could see the deep sadness in his eyes.

"I can remember my mother. She and I were living on Xora. My father had died in battle." Aziz bent down and trailed his fingers through the sand.

"It was an honorable warrior's death, but it had left us alone in a violent world. My mother tried so hard to be as hard-hearted as a Xoran, but she could not. She even changed her Tuulan name of Syla, to the Xoran name Scythia, in an attempt to fit in with the others. She was a formidable woman, but she was not as ruthless as the Xoran women." A tear fell as he continued.

"She overheard the other women plotting to kill her. They wanted to take me as their son. They thought her presence was weakening their appearance as strong warriors. Mother feared for me and thought they would change their minds and kill me also." Tasira stopped him.

"If your mother was afraid for you, why didn't she come with you to Tuulani?" she asked. Aziz took in a heavy breath.

"She had a natak that could transport one person to another location. She said the words while I held the natak. The next thing I knew, I was here. I was only five years when I arrived. The old woman took care of me until she died," he looked at Tasira. "I have been alone here ever since."

"I am here with you now. You aren't alone any longer." Tasira grabbed his large hand and kissed the palm. She got up on her knees and leaned over to kiss Aziz on the mouth. It was the sweetest moment he could ever recall. She kissed him again, deeper, and he gently placed his opposite hand around her waist and pulled her closer. He never wanted the feeling to stop, but this madness must end. She must find a male who was more like her.

There were many to choose from in the village. Aziz had seen the other males looking at Tasira. He knew he wasn't the right one for her. He was too primal in his feelings. He must show her that he was not right for her.

He would ask Seta for help. He took his hand off of her and set her back from him.

"I must go now," he said, looking at the ground. He left her kneeling in the sand, wondering what she had done wrong.

Aziz went looking for Seta, but she was busy with the Elders in some kind of meeting. He stood there for a moment and then a thought came to him. He knew what he must do to stop this from going any further. He walked quickly to his home and began to gather his things.

Tasira watched Aziz walk away from her as she knelt on the sand. She sat down wondering what had just happened. Aziz was always so quiet and distant, but she knew he enjoyed being with her on their walks. *"Why is he making this so difficult? He knows that I care for him. I told him that I wanted to be with him, so why does he run away?"* Tasira thought. Suddenly, the best reason for his behavior became very clear to her making her roll her eyes.

"He doesn't want to be with me. How could I be so dense? All I have been doing is embarrassing Aziz and making a fool of myself." Tasira rose from her place on the ground and brushed the sand off of her clothing. She went directly back to her room vowing to stop behaving

like an idiot. Tomorrow would be a better day. She would start fresh tomorrow.

Aziz was packing as much food and water as he could carry. He lived in the tiny house the old woman had raised him in and there was complete privacy for him to plan. He grabbed the old map his adoptive mother had left behind. Her mate had travelled here from another village. The writing on the map was faded, but Aziz was sure he would be able to find the place. He wrote a letter and folded it. He would leave in the evening so no one would notice. He had been a solitary man his whole life, so no one would miss him for a few days.

He sat his pack against the wall and looked for the box his second mother had cherished so much. Her mate had made the box for her and had carved every single flower in the wood himself. Aziz found the box and placed the letter inside of it. With that completed, he went outside to find Gan.

"Tinku! Stop that whining! I know you want to go and see Aziz, but you can't. He doesn't want us to bother him." Tasira was admonishing her best friend.

"What makes you think that Aziz doesn't want to see you?" Seta asked, leaning in Tasira's bedroom doorway. Tasira looked at her a little annoyed. It was bad enough to have Tinku and her own heart betraying her. She didn't really need another person questioning her actions.

"Did you hear what I asked you?" Seta asked.

"Of course, I heard you!" Tasira answered sharply and then sighed, sorry she had snapped at Seta. "I know, because he left me in the sand after I kissed him. I kind of put it all together after that. I've been an idiot and I don't want to embarrass myself or Aziz any longer. End of story, OK?"

"Have you asked him face to face if that is what was wrong? You've been in here for over three days. Don't you think you should be adult enough to at least go to speak to him?" Seta's voice began to raise. "Aziz hasn't left his house either. You two are driving me crazy!" Seta's voice was shrill with anger as she walked away. Tasira stopped for a moment and decided Seta was right.

"Seta?! Wait a moment," Tasira called after her friend, contrite, as she was walking away. Seta paused a moment, but did not turn around. Tasira ran and caught up with her.

"You're right. I should go and speak to him directly. Will you walk with me for a little while until I gather up the courage?" Tasira implored. Seta sighed, exasperated.

"Of course, I will! But *you* will go to the house yourself. Alone." Tasira nodded at Seta and gave her friend a hug. The two women left the house and walked over to the gardens.

They walked and talked for a couple of hours until Tasira finally agreed it was time for her to go to Aziz and settle this once and for all. Tasira was heading toward Aziz's home when Tul came up to her and Seta.

"Seta! Tasira! I am so glad to finally see you outside your home." Tul looked at Seta and she knew immediately that this was more than just a coincidence that he found them.

"Why are you looking for us, Tul?" Seta asked. Tul looked at Seta and motioned for them to sit on the bench by the spring.

"I'm actually looking for Tasira," he looked at her pointedly.

"For me? What can I help you with Tul?" Tasira asked puzzled.

"Gan needs to talk with you. I was told that if I saw you outside, I should bring you to him."

"Bring me to Gan? Why?" Tasira looked at Tul. Tul shrugged his shoulders.

"I don't know. He wouldn't tell me. But he did say that if Seta was with you, she should come along as well." Seta raised her eyebrows at this tidbit.

"Well Tasira, I imagine we should go with him to find out what is going on." Seta looked at Tul.

"Let's go find Gan." Tul nodded. The three of them left Aziz's walkway and continued towards the center of town.

Chapter Thirty

Aziz had been out in the desert for two days and the map he held was not as helpful as he thought it would've been. *"I should be able to get to the second oasis tomorrow. The suns are getting low. This is as good of a spot as any to rest for the night."* He took his pack off and fashioned a pillow out of his extra clothing.

He pulled out a piece of the dried meat and a few other items and prepared to eat. It didn't take long to finish the small meal, but it would be a good idea to get some extra sleep. He had been travelling almost nonstop since he left Mabray and he was feeling exhausted.

Aziz thought about Tasira and how scared she must have been to be alone out in the sands. He reached up and felt his cheek, surprised to find a tear rolling down it. How he wished he could've been the one for her, but he knew this was for the best. It was better to be miserable without her than to hurt her, as he suspected he eventually would. Another tear rolled down his cheek as he laid down on the sand to sleep.

A vague sound woke him from his sleep. Aziz was groggy and it took him a minute to realize that the clanking sound was coming from right next to him. He laid still while he slowly opened his eyes and saw two set of glowing eyes looking over at him. Two ze'evs were ransacking his rations. He either stopped them or die out here. He frowned, knowing he would die, regardless. He made a conscious decision to die fighting.

"Get out of here!" Aziz yelled in a booming voice. He quickly rose from his makeshift bed and tried to scare the thieves away. The largest one bared his teeth and lunged at Aziz. As he moved to avoid the sharp teeth, he discovered something else. There were three more sets of glowing eyes in his camp. This wasn't just a pair ze'evs. It was a pack. And they were hungry.

Aziz grabbed for the knife he had packed just as another of the ze'evs took a running leap at him. At the same time, another bit at his legs and ankles. If they succeeded in bringing Aziz down to the ground, they would rip him apart. He plunged his knife into the large female that had leaped at him and ripped her gut open. She lay dying as Aziz tried to manage to kill the two at his legs. He could feel the flesh being ripped open and he stabbed downward at the wolf-like dogs.

He could hear yipping from the ze'evs whenever he made contact with his knife. A large male leapt at him and ripped at his back. He grabbed at it and flung it to the ground. He finished killing the two on his legs and kicked his feet to get them off of him.

When Aziz stood up, he realized that the large male had moved in closer with a smaller, younger male. Aziz was bleeding profusely and the two ze'evs circled him, waiting for him to collapse. The younger male was inexperienced and impatient. It took a run at Aziz, enabling him to grab it and snap its neck. He threw the dead dog off to the side and kept his eyes on the alpha male. He would have to find a way to force it to make the first move.

He reached down and grabbed a handful of sand, threw it at the alpha, and yelled at the same time. The ze'ev dodged his feeble attempt and growled louder.

The wolf-like animal moved stealthily trying to find an opportunity to attack. Aziz tried to keep the ze'ev in front of him, but he had lost a substantial amount of blood and was feeling the effect on his body. He stumbled a bit and the ze'ev seized the opportunity.

It sunk its' teeth into his arm. Aziz yelled out in pain and stabbed at the animal. The angle was off and the knife didn't do much damage. Aziz dropped to his knees, forcing the ze'ev to let loose of his arm. It changed tactics quickly and lunged toward the Xoran's neck.

Aziz lowered his head and waited for the teeth to slip over his skull. When he could feel the ze'ev slamming into his head, he plunged the knife upward into the animal's neck. He ripped the knife through the artery, spraying blood all over. The animal fell dead on the sand and the last of Aziz's strength left him. He passed out, bleeding and alone.

Chapter Thirty-One

Tul, Seta and Tasira finally found Gan. The young man smiled at Tasira. The fleeting smile faded as he remembered his promise. This was going to break Tasira's heart. The last thing Gan wanted was to cause her pain. But he had made a promise, and he would honor it.

"Hello Tasira, Seta. I need you to come over to the table and sit down. There is something I must give to you." Gan pointed toward Tasira. "I will be back in a moment." Tasira looked at Gan as he ran the short span to his home and back. Tul put up a hand, waving off any questions.

"Before you ask me...I do not know what this is about. All I know is that I was to find you and bring you here." Tul stated. They saw Gan returning with an ornate box in his hands. It looked very old and finely crafted.

"I cannot accept a gift from you Gan. This is a beautiful heirloom and you must keep it." Tasira finished.

"Tasira, the box is not from me. Aziz made me promise to give this to you at least two evenings after I talked with him. He said that this is yours and there is a note inside." Tasira took the box out of Gan's hands. She ran her hand over the carved flowers and looked back up at Gan.

"Why can't he give this to me himself?" She looked at him with fear.

"He said you will need to read the note to understand." Gan looked at the ground, "I will leave you alone." He motioned to Tul to join him, and they walked away.

Tasira looked up at Seta who nodded at her to open the box. Inside was a folded paper. Tasira took the paper with shaking hands. Something was not right and it scared her like nothing else had before. She began to read, and her hand flew up to her mouth.

Dearest Tasira,

By the time Gan gives you this letter, I will be on my way to the other village. The woman who took care of me as a child, had a map that shows the way. I will be gone for many days by the time you get this letter, so it will be impossible to follow me.

I love you Tasira, and that is the reason I am leaving. I am Xoran and I was meant to be a warrior. Living in the village has taken some of the warrior out of me, but under it all, that is what I truly am and the killer in me begs to show itself. I saw you talking with Gan one evening and it caused a violent jealousy inside of me. I knew then that I should not continue to fantasize about us having a life together.

There are so many men in the village who want to have you as their own. I know that you would be happier and safer with one of them. You need that chance and I need to forget. I know, though, that I will continue to see you in my dreams.

Aziz

Tasira handed the letter over to Seta as she got up from the table. Seta was so intently reading that she didn't notice that Tasira had left until she was almost to the Temple. Seta knew exactly what Tasira had in mind and she was going to stop her. Seta ran as fast as she could until she reached Tasira's bedroom.

"Oh no you don't!" Seta grabbed Tasira's shoulder.

"With or without your blessing, I am going to find him. You cannot stop me, nor should you try. I will not negotiate on this. Aziz is the man I want, and I will find him even if I go out there alone." Tasira stated firmly as she packed her things for her journey.

"How in the name of the Priestess do you think you are going to do that?! We don't even know what direction he went. You would be going out there to die!" Seta was getting angry now.

"I will ask Tinku for his help. He found you here, he can find Aziz too." Tasira continued to pack. "I will need a piece of Aziz's clothing. Tinku will find him by scent."

"You are insane! There is no way that a ze'ev, no matter how smart you think he is, can find someone in the desert who has been gone for three days. This is complete madness, Tasira!" Seta yelled.

"No. It is not madness Seta," said a third female voice. "It can be done. I have Aziz's medallion, and you have yours Tasira." The old woman, Dela, held out the medallion to Tasira.

"Hold the two together," instructed Dela. "You were born with the power to see visions. That is why you are here. You followed the vision in your head." Dela nodded.

"You also have empathic powers. You made Tinku understand you. There has never been a ze'ev that could be tamed, until you came along." Dela motioned for Tasira to come to her. Tasira followed the unspoken instructions.

"Now take your medallion and Aziz's medallion and place them together in your hands. Concentrate on Aziz."

Seta looked at the two women and watched as Tasira closed her eyes and placed the medallions together in her hands. The medallions began to glow. Tasira's chin lifted violently and her back arched as if she had been stabbed through the heart.

Tasira's first vision was Aziz leaving the village and travelling out toward the setting suns. He stopped by an oasis and filled his water skin. Now, the suns were setting over his right shoulder.

The next vision was scattered. There were ze'evs, a violent fight, and blood everywhere. The last thing Tasira saw was Aziz lying on the blood-soaked sand. Tasira collapsed to her knees and the medallions fell to the floor.

"I have to go to him, he is dying. He was attacked by a pack of ze'evs." Tasira looked up at Dela with wild eyes. "Do you think anyone will go with me? I cannot carry him by myself." A small hand was offered to Tasira.

"We will ask the others. Come with me," Seta offered.

Tasira and Seta went to the large bell and rang it. Soon everyone came to the center of the village. Seta stood on the large table.

"Aziz is in the sands. He is injured and dying. Tasira is asking if anyone will go with her to bring Aziz back to us." Seta turned around to look at everyone standing there.

"Raise your hand if you are willing to go. We will need at least four volunteers." Gan raised his hand first and six other men did also. Tasira would have the help she needed. One of the women spoke up.

"We will get water and the stretcher. Go home and pack food for yourselves." Dela looked at Seta, "We will also pack bandages and medicine."

"Thank you for your help. We will leave as quickly as you can return to this spot." Tasira was crying when she went to get the pack from her room.

Chapter Thirty-Two

They had been searching all night and now the suns were beginning to rise again. They needed to find Aziz or he would surely die. One hour later, Tinku started running into the distance. The group followed as fast as they could, but the heat was already becoming intolerable.

As they came up over the dune, the oasis Tasira had seen in her vision appeared. She looked at Gan who smiled and nodded. The eight searchers stopped and filled any water skin that was not completely full. They ate a bit of their food and then they continued the search.

"Tasira, what if we cannot find him or, worse, cannot save him? What will you want us to do?" Gan asked softly, knowing that these could be real possibilities.

"I do not think the Priestess would allow me to have those visions if there wasn't a chance. I cannot think about this now. If I have to face it later, I will make the decision." Tasira fought back tears, knowing that Gan may be right. He was just trying to prepare her for the worst. She grabbed his hand.

"Thank you, Gan, for your concern. I know that you are trying to help me anyway you can." She brought her hand up to his shoulder and gently patted it. Gan smiled and went over to the others to ease their minds too.

Four hours later, they came up over a high dune and were horrified by the carnage they saw below. Aziz lay on the sand with five dead ze'evs sprawled around him. The smell was awful. This had to have happened more than a day before. Tasira took off, running down the sand, stumbling as she went, screaming Aziz's name. Gan watched her as she painfully descended the sand. He looked ahead of her and saw no movement from Aziz's body. The searchers watched as Tasira dropped next to him.

"Aziz!" Tasira screamed, "Aziz wake up." She felt his chest and there was shallow breathing.

"He is still alive! He is breathing, but he won't wake." She looked further and saw gashes and bite marks from his head down. He was covered in dried blood and she wasn't sure how much of it was his and how much was from the ze'evs. Tinku came up and licked at Aziz's face and hands, but that got no response either.

"Let's get Aziz on the stretcher and start back toward the oasis. We will stop as soon as we reach it. Tasira can attend to Aziz with the water from the spring." Gan called out to the others and helped them ready Aziz for the four-hour trek to the oasis. Tasira gathered what she could of Aziz's belongings and put them in his pack.

The group arrived at the oasis almost six hours later. It had been more difficult to carry Aziz than they had first thought. They had stopped frequently to change who was carrying the stretcher and to drink water.

But now, they were here and would rest most of the night. They would leave before the suns rose again to travel a short time in the cool night air.

Tasira had finished carrying water over to the men and then to Aziz to clean his body. It would take a while to complete the task since his wounds would also have to be stitched.

"Aziz, it's Tasira. I'm going to be cleaning the blood off of you and it may hurt," she paused, "I will also have to stitch some of your wounds because they are deep. I will place b'nat root on your wound to help with the pain. OK?" Gan noticed that Tasira kept talking to Aziz even though he did not respond. She wanted him to hear her voice.

Gan almost wished it was he who was laying on the sand. Her hands so carefully touching him. But, would've never left a female who was that devoted to him. He had never seen a love so fierce before. Aziz was a fool for not seeing it.

Tasira started with Aziz's face. As she washed the blood away, she smiled at the rugged face she had grown to love. She cleaned his forehead and prepared to stitch the first of many gashes.

"Aziz. I am going to cut off the rest of your shirt and replace it with a clean one. And then I am going to have one of the men help me cut your pants above where the wounds are. When we are done, I will cover you with a sheet so you will not burn in the sun." Tasira looked over at Gan and sighed deeply as a tear rolled down her face. He nodded back to her and brought over his knife so she could begin.

Aziz was playing in the grass with some children. They were all giggling as he pretended to chase them around the tree and back out into grass once again. He smiled at them, but then they started to cry. He turned around and could see the wild ze'evs coming toward them.

He gathered the children in his arms and started running toward the house in the distance. As he got closer, he could see Tasira at the door waiting for him. He ran as fast as he could.

Now, he was inside the house. The children were walking down the hallway to go to bed. *"Good night, Papa,"* he heard the children call out. He turned around and realized that they were not talking to him. There was a man he didn't know standing next to Tasira.

The man and Tasira were smiling at the children. *"Good night,"* the man called out. He placed an arm around Tasira and she smiled at him as they made their way down the hallway. He watched, sad in the knowledge that it would never be him. His vision became blurry as his eyes welled up with tears. He wanted to tell her that he had changed his mind. But it was too late. His mind went blank again.

Tasira finished cleaning Aziz and removing the bloody garments. She had bandaged the wounds and placed the sheet over him. She was readying herself to rest a few hours when she saw a tear in the corner of his eye. She touched it and it went a short way down his cheek. She grabbed his hand and held it in hers. His hand was so large that it could have reached around both of hers and still have room. She had never considered how profoundly out of place he must have felt in the village. Tasira knew that everyone in the village was friendly to Aziz, but he always seemed to stay out of the main life of Mabray. He was the only Xoran there. His race had a reputation of being fierce and ruthless. Perhaps they had been afraid of him all along.

Gan watched Tasira as she held Aziz's hand. She held her hand inside his and measured the size. He could see the tenderness in her face and the way she touched him. So, it was no surprise that she moved her things and laid down next to Aziz. It wasn't exactly proper, but there was no harm in what she did. Gan watched as she fell asleep, the moons were shining brightly and a bright moonbeam fell across the two bodies lying together.

A second glow began between Aziz and Tasira. It rose and hovered just above their bodies. It was then that he could see it was a medallion. A woman's medallion. And he knew what that would mean. Aziz would be healed, at least in some small measure, and Tasira would have him back. Gan closed his eyes and wondered to himself if he should tell her, or just leave the incident a secret between him and the Priestess. *"A secret it shall be,"* he thought as he rolled over and fell into an exhausted sleep.

Chapter Thirty Three

The group had left the oasis early and was back in the village by the end of the day. Everyone turned out to see if they had found Aziz. Most were shocked to see that he still lived.

They moved him to the Temple so that Tasira could tend to him. The older women came in and removed all of his clothing and finished cleaning him with cool water. They changed his bandages and put new clothing on Aziz. Tasira waited outside until they were finished. One of the women wiped her hands dry as she walked out.

"It is a good thing that there were a number of us around. That man is heavy!" She smiled at Tasira and patted her shoulder. "We will come and check on him every day until he awakens. If you need help, just send someone to tell us and we will be here."

Every day the women did as they promised and every night Tasira slept in the chair in Aziz's room. On the fourth day, Tasira was exhausted, but she went to Aziz's room to sleep in the chair.

"You need to sleep in your own bed Tasira," Seta stated as she stood at the foot of Aziz's bed. "You will become ill if you do not take better care of yourself."

"I am fine Seta. You need not worry. As soon as Aziz wakes up, I will sleep more and eat better. You will see, everything will be back to normal." Tasira smiled at Seta. Seta shook her head and walked away. There was no way to force her to sleep or eat. The woman was just too stubborn, and her worry too deep. Tasira turned her attention toward Aziz.

"I am back with you again. If you need anything, you will have to wake up and let me know." She moved the large chair next to the bed and sat down. She grabbed Aziz's hand and looked over at him with tears in her eyes.

"Please wake up Aziz. I want you here with me." Tasira snuggled down in the chair and continued to hold Aziz's hand. She finally fell into a deep, exhausted sleep and the world went completely dark.

The light was beginning to come into the room and Aziz squinted as he tried to open his eyes. Slowly the light became more bearable and he saw that he was in a bed. He looked a little further over, and saw Tasira in the chair next to him. She was holding his hand and sleeping so soundly. She looked as though she hadn't slept in a week, but she was so beautiful to him. He closed his eyes again, angry that his efforts had been for nothing. He was right back where he had started. *"Why? Why did I have to be found? I would have been out of my misery and out of her life forever. How did I get back here?"* The flood of questions spun through his head. Tasira moved a little. He opened his eyes and looked down at her once more. This was going to be difficult.

"Tasira...Tasira wake up," his voice cracked a little. But soon, she was opening her eyes.

"Aziz? Oh, thank the Priestess! You are awake." Tasira reached over and caressed his cheek. He caught her hand and put it back down by her side. She looked at him, hurt by his coldness.

"Please go and get Seta. I want to speak to her." Aziz finished the statement flatly and closed his eyes. Tasira looked at him oddly as a tear slipped down her cheek. She looked down at the floor and went to find her friend, Seta. Maybe she could figure this out.

"Aziz wants to speak to you." Tasira blurted out. Seta looked at her with raised eyebrows.

"He wants to speak to *me?*" Seta asked, shocked. Seta looked at the woman who went into the sands and retrieved Aziz, who got seven others to go with her, for a vision that no one else had seen. And then, upon their return, spent her following days by his side. Seta could feel the hurt that Tasira was holding inside of her. Aziz must have said something else to her.

"What did he say to you, Tasira, when he awoke? Seta tried to ask nonchalantly.

"He said nothing else," Tasira's chin wavered slightly. "He only said that he wanted to speak to you." Tasira turned around and went to her room. She shut the door quietly, but Aziz could hear her crying in the adjoining room.

Seta walked the short distance to the room where Aziz was laying. He was awake, but his wounds were still visible. They were healing, without being bandaged. He looked tired and upset. Seta walked over to the bed and sat in the chair next to it.

"You asked to speak with me, Aziz?" Seta spoke with no emotion in her face. Underneath it all, however, she was afraid of what he would say next.

"Yes, Seta," he nodded, eyes flashing. "I want to know why I am back here!" Aziz looked at Seta as he continued in a harsh whisper.

"I left this village for a reason, and you know what it is. You have always known why I live the way I do. Always here, but never a part of anything." He looked sideways at the sounds he heard coming from the next room and nodded his head towards the soft sobs.

"The pain Tasira feels is nothing compared to the pain I would cause her later." Aziz paused and looked at the wounds on his legs. "Tell me what has happened to me. All I can remember is that I was attacked by a pack of ze'evs. The next thing I remember is falling to the sands." Aziz looked up at Seta.

"Then I wake up here, and Tasira is by my side." He looked at Seta with anger, "Who would allow her to be alone with me in here. She should have been encouraged to stay away. You should have ordered her to stay away!" Seta, who had always been a calm, even-tempered person, lost her temper for the first time since she was a child.

"Order her to stay away?! That is what you think I should have done, is it?" Seta whispered back angrily.

"That young woman in the next room has been though more than you know! She has every right to be in here with you!" Seta hit him hard on the arm, and the big man winced.

"It was Tasira who wanted to find you. She had a vision of where to go in the sands and was ready to leave the village alone if necessary. Seven men volunteered when they saw her determination. In part, I'm sure, that they wished that it could be one of them. But it was you she sought." She took a moment to subdue her heated anger.

"She found you rotting in a pool of your own blood, in the blistering heat of the suns, with the bloated carcasses of the ze'evs you had killed. I hear it was quite a gory site and smelled like death." Seta paused for a moment and watched the Xoran's face intently.

"But even after seeing the bloody mess, do you know what she did? She ran down to you without a second thought and brought you back here in the hopes that you would recover." Seta hit him again.

"That young woman may be small of stature, but she has the heart of a warrior. You, Aziz, are just so used to feeling sorry for yourself that you cannot see it." Seta started walking out of the room.

"Is there anything else?" Seta asked with her back turned. Aziz's eyes flashed with stubbornness.

"Yes. I can still choose who attends to my wounds and where that happens, correct?" Aziz asked. Seta nodded. "Then I will be moving to my house and I will call for help if I need it. Is that understood?" Seta looked at him and then motioned to Gan, who was coming down the hall.

"Gan, Aziz is awake and wants to go to his home." She looked up at the handsome young man. "He wants to be in complete control of who helps him and where he is living. I want no more of this behavior. Please take him home." Seta finished and walked past Gan.

The young man looked after Seta with his mouth partially open. He couldn't form a word, much less an intelligent question. He shook his head and walked past a closed door where he could hear crying. Then he entered the room Aziz had been placed in. What in the name of the dypul was happening here? It certainly wasn't the work of the Priestess.

Chapter Thirty-Four

A couple of days went by and Gan continued to look after Aziz. The Xoran was silent most of the time and completely intolerable the rest. It finally got to be too much for Dela, the old woman who was helping him. No one had ever heard her say much, but when she did, you had better listen.

Dela came to help him for the third day. Aziz was in a foul mood and told the old woman to leave. Dela nodded and picked up her things. She was making her way to the door, when she turned around and looked at the two men in the room. The oversized Xoran and the smaller Tuulan. She pointed to Gan and crooked her finger for him to follow her. Then she took one last look at Aziz, pointing to him.

"You are possibly the most dim-witted man I have ever met. You take out your pain on others who try to help you. The ones who love you. You will regret your life if you do not change soon." Dela finished and nodded her head for emphasis. She turned and walked through the doorway with Gan close behind her. He had offered to help carry her supplies, but she just pulled them away from his reach.

There was no way he would pick a fight with this woman. She kind of scared him to be honest. Dela stopped outside the door, by the trees and turned around. Gan almost ran into her as he followed.

"Aziz needs to be left alone now. He needs to feel alone. Do you understand me?" Dela looked at Gan with her head cocked sideways.

"Tasira is the one who needs you now. She is in love with Aziz. But...*that man* needs to know that he has competition." Dela pointed to Aziz's home to emphasize her words. "I have seen the way Tasira looks at you. She is grateful, that is all. But she could learn to feel more than that if Aziz leaves her again. Do you understand my meaning?" Gan looked at the old woman and nodded. He would gladly walk about town with Tasira on his arm. Even if it was only to make his friend come to his senses. He would try not to hope too much that Aziz stayed as brainless as Dela implied.

It had been over two weeks since Aziz had left the Temple. Seta watched as Tasira tried to go out and play with the young ones after their studies. No matter how hard she tried, Tasira could not completely herself.

Her laughter was no longer as infectious as it had once been. Things had gotten some better since Gan showed up to ask Tasira out for a walk, but progress was slow. It would take her a little while to decide what to do next.

Tasira watched as Gan walked across the center of the village. He had been so kind to her since Aziz had left the Hall, but she was afraid that he would get the wrong impression. She decided she would talk to him tonight about that. With that settled, she smiled as he walked up to her.

"Hello, Tasira," Gan smiled back. He was quite handsome and Tasira knew that there were other females who thought the same.

"Hello, Gan. Would you care to go for a walk with me?"

"That's why I am here. I was going to ask you the same question." Gan smiled broadly. "Where shall we go, Tasira?"

"Anywhere you like, Gan. It is a beautiful night and there is nowhere I can think of that would not make for a wonderful evening." Gan smiled at her again.

He hoped that he did not look nervous as he took her hand and placed it in the crook of his arm. He knew Aziz watched him. He had cornered Gan the night before, asking questions about his relationship with Tasira. Relationship? Gan didn't even know that he and Tasira had one, but apparently the big Xoran thought so. He certainly wasn't going to argue the point with him.

He smiled again, and took Tasira off toward the spring. He knew it was one of her favorite spots in the village.

Aziz watched them as they walked and talked. Tasira laughed at something Gan had said and the sound of her laughter rang in Aziz's ears. It was painful to see her falling in love with Gan. It should have been him, but he knew he should not think things like that.

Still, he was jealous of the time Gan spent with her and wondered if he would ever find another woman like Tasira. He doubted it. Tasira was beyond extraordinary.

Aziz watched as they sat down by the spring and snuggled together. He could hear Gan say something to her and then Tasira's voice reply. The suns were almost completely down on the horizon when he saw Tasira place her hand on Gan's cheek and kiss him, eyes closed and mouth slightly open.

He looked at Gan and saw the young Tuulan place a hand around her waist and pull her a little closer. As they got up from their spot at the spring, they walked hand-in-hand to a variety of other quiet spots and then returned to the Temple. As Gan walked inside the building, Aziz couldn't take it any longer. He went home to sit in the darkness.

Tasira and Gan left the Temple and walked toward the spring. She knew that he brought her here because it was her favorite. She may not love this young man, but she could certainly get used to being treated so well.

"Gan, you and I need to talk. Shall we sit down?" Tasira motioned toward the bench. Gan nodded, knowing what she was going to say. Wanting to ease her mind, he started the conversation.

"Tasira, I also need to tell you something and I need you to listen to me first. OK?" Gan looked at her in a meaningful way that made Tasira suspect that there was more going on than she knew. Tasira nodded, and he continued. "While I tell you everything, I need you to snuggle up close to me. Can you do that?"

"Of course, Gan," Tasira stated and then leaned over to whisper in Gan's ear. "You are doing this for the benefit of Aziz, aren't you?" She looked the shocked young man in the eyes.

"He watches us, doesn't he?" Gan nodded at her, his smile widening to show bright white, perfect teeth. "So, tell me about this plan. Who put you up to this idea?"

"Dela," Gan continued to smile. "She believes that Aziz needs to be jolted into understanding what he is throwing away." His smile faded, "She also thinks that if he goes away forever, that it would be a good thing to have a friend around to help you."

"I am trying *not* to hope that he goes away. That is a terrible thing, I assure you." Gan looked up at Tasira with twinkling eyes. Tasira laughed delightedly at Gan.

"You are completely without shame, Gan!" Tasira laughed again. "And so am I," she whispered and placed her hand on Gan's face. She drew him nearer, parting her lips ever so slightly and kissing him in a way that left no question as to it meaning.

Gan was taken by complete surprise by Tasira's astute comprehension of his visits. More importantly, he was surprised she would kiss him in such a way. As the kiss continued, he instinctively drew her nearer to him, wanting more. He knew Aziz would be insanely jealous, but at this moment, he did not care. The kiss lasted a short moment longer, allowing Gan to take control of his senses. He looked at Tasira, her eyes still closed. As she opened them, she looked back at him, making it quite clear that she had felt something too.

"I must be careful not to do such things. It is not fair." Tasira said softly. Gan could see that she was ashamed that she might give him the wrong idea.

"I will take my chances, Tasira. I know what the game is. But there are still two possible outcomes, aren't there." Gan whispered with a smile and gave Tasira a hand up as they continued on their evening walk.

Chapter Thirty-Five

The ritual had continued for a number of evenings. Aziz continued to watch from the shadows although he did not know why. This evening had been so painful he hurt in his chest. A dagger was stabbing him, he was almost sure of it. He went back home, to his dark little house, alone as always.

"I trusted him and he falls in love with the only woman who ever cared for me." Aziz shook that thought out of his head. It was not fair to blame Gan, he knew Aziz did not want to pursue Tasira. Still, it hurt more than any of the wounds he had ever gotten.

"I cannot continue to do this. I will be in pain forever, just as Dela had said. And it is my own fault." Aziz closed his eyes in pain.

"But how can I continue to dream of a woman I cannot have? My heart must have the pain taken from it. I

will talk to Seta tomorrow morning, as the suns rise, and ask her to help cure me of this pain. The Temple of Kala and the medallion should have that power." He paused for a moment and then reached for a piece of paper. He would also write Tasira a letter to tell her that he no longer wanted her. Aziz nodded. This was going to make tomorrow a better day. He exhaled sadly when the note was written. He laid on the counter next to the door and went to bed. Tomorrow was the day.

Tasira and Gan had completed their walk for the last time. She was going to confront Aziz tomorrow. Only after she knew for sure could she plan what path her life would take.

Gan looked at her, smiled a little, and told her he understood. No matter what he wanted, it would be up to Tasira to give her heart to the man she loved. No one could choose for her, and he would not stand in her way.

"Thank you for helping me and being there for me when I needed you," Tasira smiled as a tear fell down her face. "You are a very good man and any woman would be happy with you as their mate." Gan smiled again.

"Not every woman though." He looked at her once more. "Please consider me if you have a change of heart, Tasira." Gan gently placed his hands on her arms. "At least tell me I will be the man you come to if he turns you away forever." Tasira rubbed his cheek and reached up to give him a quick kiss.

"Of course," she stated as she turned into the Hall and walked away. He watched her as she walked away, knowing that he had tasted his last kiss from her.

She could hear Seta's distinctive steps coming towards her room. She smiled and got up to meet her friend at her doorway. Seta looked very sad as she came closer. There was something on her mind and it weighed on her heavily.

"Good Morning Tasira," she said in a carefully metered voice. "There is something I need to speak to you about," Seta said with a sigh. She knew this would break Tasira's heart after all of the work she had done to encourage Aziz to realize his feelings for her. It had been difficult watching Tasira and Gan go out every evening for a walk. She knew that they were putting on a show for Aziz. Apparently, the outcome was the opposite of what they had intended.

"What is it, Seta?" Tasira asked warily. Seta looked at the tile on the floor.

"It is about Aziz," Seta started, but was interrupted.

"Good! I've been looking for him everywhere... "Tasira's stopped short. Seta was holding up her hand. A silent plea for Tasira to stop talking. Seta looked at her new friend and hoped that she was a strong woman. It would be the only way to get through this.

"That is what I wish to talk to you about this morning," Seta explained. "And no more interrupting until I am through, OK?" Tasira nodded her head slowly a little afraid of what Seta was going to tell her. Seta continued.

"Aziz came to speak to me early this morning. He wanted me to remove the pain he was having. But I couldn't. I cannot remove the kind of pain he has unless there is a bonding involved. That is just not the case in this instance." Seta paused to let what she had just told Tasira sink in.

"He has always been in love with you Tasira. It's just that he is a complicated man and he does not know anything about how love works. Do you understand what I am trying to say?" Seta looked at Tasira. Tasira shook her head. She was going to have to tell her the parts of the story that she knew.

"Aziz has told you that he came here as a young child?" Tasira nodded. Seta continued, "Alright." She metered her words as she told the story.

"Try to imagine how abandoned he felt. How different he was from the rest." Seta sighed. "Aziz had no family and there was no one like him in the village. He scared the others with his size and his Xoran lineage. Even as a child." Seta tried to find the right words.

"He has never been with a woman, except once. But she left him for another." A tear fell down Seta's face in empathy.

"She and Aziz had been a couple for a couple of weeks and he had asked me to bond them. She refused to see him and then announced that she had found another Tuulan who would bond with her. They left this place to be away from him. No one knows if they survived or not." Tasira's friend looked at her, trying to convey the depth of loss she was feeling for Aziz.

"He was abandoned. Again." Seta swallowed hard, knowing she was telling a story that was not hers to explain.

"He has never loved anyone the way he loves you. Not even the one before you. He says he does not want you, because he is protecting you. But...I think he is protecting himself. He is more sensitive than he shows and his heart cannot handle any more pain. He has resigned himself to a life of self-imposed isolation. To protect you." Tasira nodded, but Seta thought she needed to clarify a few things.

"Aziz was afraid of what might happen if he continued to be around you. That is why he left the village and why he is doing this now." Seta looked at the confused Tasira and sighed.

"You know he is Xoran, yes?" Seta waited for Tasira to nod. Seta looked at the innocent and inexperienced woman in front of her. She wasn't sure how to explain details to a virgin female. Seta straightened herself and tried to prepare an explanation.

"The Xoran males can be very…um…robust in their desires. Do you understand what I am saying?" Tasira looked even more confused than she had previously. Seta sighed again. She wished that Tasira had been mated before as she had been. The subject would not be so difficult to explain to a more experienced female. Seta took a big breath and looked at Tasira, deciding on how to best start over in her explanation.

"Aziz is afraid that he will hurt you if he bonds with you. He is a very large male and he is afraid of hurting you." She looked directly at Tasira. Now the young female was beginning to understand.

"He told me that he would rather spend his life alone than ever hurt you. He loves you that much, Tasira. And, he doesn't want to be near you again. He said that he cannot guarantee he will not lose control."

Seta watched the young Tuulan closely. She could see that her mind was trying to make sense out of everything. She also saw that the sweet, young woman's hidden temper was rearing its ugly head. This made Seta smile. She knew Tasira was only beginning to work up to a full-blown explosion.

"So…Aziz thinks he is the only one with a say in this?" Tasira's voice got louder as she spoke.

"I imagine he told you that I should be mated with Gan as soon as possible?" Tasira snapped a look at Seta. Seta nodded and smiled. This was going to be a full explosion.

"I go out into the sands for this man, risk everything for him and he doesn't even say thank you?" Tasira paced, arms folded.

"I love him, he loves me, and he still has no idea that he has no choice? If he loves me then we should be together." Tasira grabbed her shoes and walked toward the door.

"He will have to tell me to my face that he does not want me. We will see what he has to say to that!" Seta looked at Tasira. She had an emotional depth that surprised Seta.

This was going to be good for both of them. Seta stepped out of Tasira's way. She wasn't even thinking of stopping her. Aziz had been alone far too long and Tasira was just the woman to show him he could be happy. She wasn't afraid of what he might do, but Seta was pretty sure that Aziz should be afraid of what Tasira had in mind if he resisted her.

"Have you seen Aziz?" Tasira pointed at Hani. The startled man shook his head. This same question was asked over and over until she found the old, smiling female named Dela.

"Yes, Tasira. I have seen him," she said and then turned her face away from Tasira. Tasira went around to Dela's face and kneeled in front of her.

"Please tell me where he is. I need to talk to him." Tasira asked respectfully, holding the old woman's hands. Dela pointed at the tall cliff behind her.

"Be careful, the rock is treacherous and it is a long climb to the top. But I hear the view is worth the effort." Dela winked at Tasira and she smiled back.

Chapter Thirty-Six

Tasira hated heights. She looked up at the sheer incline and swallowed hard. She closed her eyes and took a deep breath to center herself, to prepare for the climb. Then, just as quickly, she opened her eyes and kissed Dela on the cheek. The old woman chuckled and shook her head at the foolishness of young people.

The first few hundred feet was not difficult but the next two hundred was going to take some effort. Tasira climbed and pulled herself up on the next shelf and then the next. Soon it was only a series of footholds and narrow crevices to help Tasira ascend toward the top. Her fear had long since faded into determination, and she conquered the last few steps without thought. As she got to the top of the big rock, she saw Aziz sitting on the edge of the other side.

"Aziz," Tasira breathed out his name heavily. He flinched a little, but did not say anything. Tasira walked closer and then stopped.

"You are not welcome here Tasira. I want to be alone." Aziz said in a terse voice. He didn't turn to face her.

"I don't believe you, Aziz." Tasira answered. She dragged her foot across the dirt below her.

"I spoke to Seta this morning," Tasira paused, "She told me what you had said to her. And why." She walked up behind him, slowly moving toward the man that she longed to be with. She reached him, finally, and touched Aziz on his shoulders.

"Did you think that I would be afraid of you? Don't you realize I'm not the type to be scared, not anymore." Tasira place her cheek next to his as she leaned over his shoulders. Aziz grabbed her, fiercely, and pinned her arms with one hand.

"I don't think you understand, Tasira," he spoke to her with an edge to his voice. "I am not like you, I am a Xoran. I cannot mate with anyone as small as you." He closed his eyes in pain, loosening his grip a little.

"I'm always on the edge of being a warrior, and regardless of how much I want to change, I cannot. I do not want to hurt you." Aziz finished, letting go of her wrists and walking away in shame. "I have never wanted to be something other than I am, more than I do right now."

Tasira walked after him and made him turn around and sit on a large rock. He was in so much pain that the feeling hit Tasira in the chest. It was almost too much pain to bear. She knew how he ached inside from being different and it replaced her anger with tenderness.

"Aziz, I do not want you to be anything or anyone but who you are right now. You are not as barbaric as you think you are, you know." Tasira cupped his face in her hands and tried to wipe the tears away.

"I am not afraid of you and I would never be afraid of you." She made him look at her. "I need to tell you a story. Will you listen to me?" Aziz nodded his head. Tasira continued.

"Back on Earth, where I was born, the Tuulans were hunted until they were almost extinct. The village where my Father's people lived was the last of its kind. They were the last Tuulans left." Tasira paused and looked at Aziz.

"My father was sent on a quest to find a female who would bond with him. He always says he thought it was a fool's errand because he was so large and most Human females were small compared to other Tuulans." Tasira smiled. "My father isn't like other Tuulans. He is much larger." Tasira stroked Aziz's cheek.

"He feared that his size would only intimidate a Human further. In addition, he was to find the female that was in our legends. The one who would "save the Tuulans." Tasira emphasized the phrase by holding her hands up to the sky, smirking a bit at the overly-dramatic phrase. Tasira looked at Aziz again and saw that he was entranced by the story that seemed to mirror his own life. Tasira continued with her story.

"Instead, Mother saved Father." Aziz looked dubious. Tasira sniffed in indignation. "It is true. She saved him from a large pit meant to trap Tuulans. She had never seen a Tuulan before and was a little scared because of the stories she had been told." Tasira looked at Aziz in his eyes, seeing that his moment of disbelief had been replaced by respect. Respect for Tasira's mother.

"But she pulled my father out of the pit anyway. He could have snapped her neck like a dry piece of wood. But he didn't." She grabbed his face and made Aziz look at her again.

"But he didn't." Tasira repeated louder.

"They fell in love and had me and my other siblings, Tamara and Nathaniel. My mother not only survived the mating with a male much larger that she was, but she had three babes at one time." She looked at him again. Aziz looked at her confused.

"I thought Tuulans could not survive multiple births. Either the mother dies, or the babe dies, right?" He asked, looking confused. Tasira looked at him and smiled.

"Not my mother. She had another pregnancy and had twins. Telora and Ketasha." He looked at her, not knowing whether or not to believe her. Tasira nodded again.

"It is true, Aziz. It is love that matters, not the differences between two people. As long as they love each other and do not care what others think, they will be together until they pass though the veil." Tasira leaned over and kissed him.

"Do you understand what I am telling you?" Tasira kissed him again. "I don't want another mate. I want to be with you. But, if you say no and can tell me that you do not have feelings for me, I will respect your wishes and leave you alone." She looked at him in the eyes once more. Aziz stared at her, silent. She was tired of waiting.

"Look at me and tell me you do not have feelings for me. Look me directly in the eye and say it." Tasira dared him. "Look me in the eye and say that you do not want me to be your mate!" She escalated the dare. Aziz could not do it.

"This is why I left. I did not want you to find me. I cannot say those things to you Tasira." Aziz looked at her, scared to death. "I love you. That is why I didn't want you to find me." He looked at her. "I did not think you would find me up here." Tasira chuckled.

"Did you think that I would let this rock stand between me and you? I didn't let the sands come between us, so why would I let this? When a woman in my family decides that she wants to be bonded with a particular male, the only thing that will stop her is if he tells her that he doesn't want the same thing." She finished with a smile. Aziz smiled back, showing his shining, white teeth for the first time. Tasira ran toward him and jumped up to put her arms around his neck. She kissed him and he held her close to him. He looked down at her and could see that she was nervous.

"Have you changed your mind, Tasira. It is alright if you did," he looked at her with concern. She looked at him and blushed a little.

"It is that I have never been with a man before. I know what will happen, I have read about mating, but I have never…um…experienced it before." Aziz smiled at her shyness.

"We will not be doing anything until we have been bonded in front of our friends, as is proper." He smiled broadly at her, "But that does not mean we cannot do more of this until that happens," and he kissed her again.

A couple of hours later, the two of them returned to the village. They walked into the town, hand in hand. Their friends clapped and congratulated them. They walked up to the Temple of Kala where Seta and Tasira had been living. Seta came out with a smile on her face.

"You know...she bullied everyone in the town until she found where you had gone. I pity you if she ever gets angry with you!" Seta teased Aziz. He blushed a bit as he smiled.

"I'll take my chances, Seta." he said to her as he smiled widely. Seta looked at him strangely, she had never seen the Xoran smile so brightly before. Tasira was definitely the best thing that had happened to both him and this village.

"Tasira and I wish to be bonded in front of our friends, don't we Tasira?" Aziz looked at Tasira tenderly. Tasira nodded.

"We want to be together as mates, Seta." Tasira replied, looking at her soon-to-be husband. Seta nodded at the two of them. Seta turned her attention to the gathering group behind them.

"Let us ready for a bonding ceremony tonight. We will feast and wish the couple well." She walked around to everyone and whispered instructions to each of them. This was going to be a party to remember.

Within the hour, the old woman, Dela came into Tasira's room. She gave her a beautiful blue dress. "This was mine when I was young. My mate and I had seventy-eight years together. I wait for my turn to pass though the veil to be with him once again." Tasira smiled and thanked her. Dela nodded.

"Be happy, enjoy *your* next seventy-eight years. Love him and cherish him. There will be a time when you wished you had said more. Time runs out for us all. But for tonight, you are the owner of time. This is your night to remember in the years to come." Dela hugged the young woman and smiled. Then she disappeared. Seta watched as the old woman walked away.

"That is the first time I can ever remember Dela speaking more than a few words to anyone. She hasn't spoken to anyone, really, since her mate died three years ago." Seta looked at Tasira.

"She helped me find Aziz in the sands, and told me how to find Aziz today. She was the only one who would tell me anything." Tasira said, finding this set of coincidences as amazing as Seta did.

Both women felt that there were things that happened in their lives that were meant steer them in the right direction. All they needed to do was pay attention and say thank you when the gift was given.

Chapter Thirty-Seven

As the suns hung just above the sands, the last of the preparations were made. Neither Aziz or Tasira had been allowed to see what was happening outside their rooms. As they were led outside, and brought together, they looked around at the party that had been made for them.

There were flowers at the altar, a bottle of A'vata nectar, and a meal waited on the stone table outside the Great Hall. There were lanterns hanging around the altar and their friends were all seated on chairs in a semi-circle around them. They were all smiling as Aziz took Tasira's hand and led her to the altar. Seta stood across the other side of the stone platform and asked them both to kneel.

"Tasira do you give yourself willingly to Aziz?" Seta asked her.

"Yes, I give myself willingly to Aziz," Tasira stated with sincerity.

"Aziz do you give yourself willingly to Tasira?" Seta turn her attention to Aziz.

"Yes. I give myself willingly to Tasira," Aziz pledged as he looked at Tasira.

Seta took out Aziz's medallion from a beautiful case. She gave it to Aziz and he placed it around his neck. He closed his eyes and started saying the promise.

"*Hirsa ke bakt te. Su'un Tasira te me la hibbay. Tasira te la hibbay la'alam,*" Aziz finished. He placed the medallion around Tasira's neck and held her hands. Tasira spoke the promise next.

"*Hirsa ke bakt te, Ga'bara Aziz te me la hibbay. Aziz te la hibbay la'alam,*" finished Tasira. She reached for Aziz's face and drew him close to her. As they kissed, a golden glow enveloped the two of them and touched nothing else. They could see only each other and the rest of the world faded away. When the kiss ended, they looked around and slowly the crowd around them came back into focus. Seta was the first to speak to them.

"That was some kiss. Time seemed to stop for you two. I have never seen anything like it before." Seta said in a breathless voice. They nodded to her and got up to take part in the feast after the bonding.

Tasira could not have imagined that her feelings would deepen so profoundly. Aziz looked at Tasira as if he felt the same way. They held hands and ate their food with the other. When they had spent the appropriate amount of time at the party, they excused themselves and went into Tasira's room. Seta watched them and smiled as they walked away.

Tasira's room had been decorated with presents from the rest of the village as was the custom for bondings and births. But Aziz and Tasira barely noticed.

"I don't know where to begin, Aziz. I don't know how to make this special for you." Tasira said, avoiding his eyes. Aziz put a finger under her chin and she looked up at him.

"I never thought I would be bonded with anyone, and you are so beautiful. Even if we just lay next to each other, I will be fortunate to experience this closeness with you." Aziz smiled at her. He was determined to be as gentle as he could, but being so close to her without touching her was a pleasurable torture. He knew there would be a time he would not be able to stop his body from betraying him, but for now, he wanted Tasira to feel safe and loved.

Tasira stood on the small wooden step in front of her bed and began taking off Aziz's shirt. Her fingers softly brushed across his chest as she opened the buttons of his shirt. His chest and torso were bare against her hands and her long, black hair brushed softly against him. She stopped for a moment when she saw the new scars. She wanted to soothe them away. Tasira softly brushed her fingers across the healing wounds. He closed his eyes at the pleasure of it, his breathing quickened. He had never felt so completely loved before. Tasira placed her face against him and listened to his heartbeat. She would never tire of that sound.

Tasira raised her head and looked at Aziz as she brushed his shirt over his shoulders until it fell to the floor. She reached up and kissed Aziz. Her mouth touched lightly, first, and then deepened as the kiss continued. She withdrew and looked up at him without saying a word. He sighed and caught his breath as he looked at her. He couldn't help himself. He drew her nearer and kissed her again until she gently pulled back.

Tasira turned around and lifted her hair for him to open the back of her dress. The buttons were small and with his nervousness it took a while for his large hands to undo all eight of them. When he had finished, Tasira turned around and shrugged the dress off her shoulders and let it fall to the floor. She stood in front of Aziz in her undergarment and began opening the buttons on Aziz's pants. When she had undone them all, Aziz helped take them off. The last thing to go was the lingerie she had been given for the wedding night. The thin straps fell over Tasira's shoulders and she let the silky material slide down across her breasts and down to the floor where she stepped over it into Aziz's arms.

Tasira ran her fingers across his skin. His chest felt so warm and she could feel his heart beating. She kissed his chest and looked up to his face. Aziz's eyes were closed. Tasira took a second to look at him fully, remembering the advice that Dela had given her. She wanted this day to be in her mind forever. Aziz opened his eyes and looked down at the loving look he was receiving from Tasira.

"It is alright if you are afraid Tasira. We can wait. I do not want to hurt or scare you. Everything will happen in its own time." Aziz was gentle and tender. Tasira looked at him and ran her hands up his arms to his shoulders.

"I am not afraid. I was just remembering Dela's advice. I am building memories of you and me and our first night together as husband and wife." Aziz looked down at her, picked her up lovingly and placed her on the bed. He laid down next to her and kissed her passionately.

Aziz ran his hand down her body and felt her soft skin. It was like nothing else he had ever felt before. "Your skin is so soft." Aziz spoke softly as he continued to stroke her skin. Tasira rolled over on her side and he put his large arm around her. She pushed herself up and leaned over to kiss Aziz. As she kissed him, his arm around her tightened, holding her close, pushing her body into his.

Tasira's hand moved effortlessly across Aziz's chest until she reached across him completely and could pull herself on top of him.

Aziz was trying not to lose control of his emotions, but Tasira's touch made him warm with desire. She was on top of him now and Aziz was feeling the frenzy of his need take control. He grabbed her slim body and quickly switched places with her. He was on top of her, tasting every part of her body. He stopped for a moment to gather his senses. His breathing was heavy as he looked into her eyes.

His eyes opened and focused on Tasira. A deep smokiness in his dark amber eyes showed the amount of restraint he was wielding in the attempt to stop himself.

Tasira watched the effort he was expending to control his body, but it had already betrayed him. She knew why he had resisted. He was afraid he would hurt her. She was the first Tuulan female who had spoken to him in a genuine manner. The time they had spent together was as comfortable as speaking to anyone she loved. It didn't take her long to realize she was in love with the Xoran, and she knew that would never change.

"I know that you think I need to be protected from you, but, I don't." Tasira looked at Aziz. "I want to make our bonding complete." She kissed his expansive chest.

Looking down at his new wife, he was entranced. This beautiful woman loved him. Tasira's last words were his undoing. Aziz kissed her, at first gently, and then more passionately. Soon the Xoran could not hold back.

Aziz wrestled with his conscience for a moment, until Tasira looked at him. Taking a deep breath, she nodded at Aziz. He looked terrified and sad.

"Tasira, there is going to be pain at first." Aziz looked at her. "Do you understand? There is going to be more pain than you have ever experienced before. Stories about this do not prepare you for the first time. I will go as slowly as I can." Tasira nodded to him. Aziz positioned himself above her. He closed his eyes for a moment before he began. He worried that he would hurt her so profoundly that she would never want to be with him again.

Tasira felt the searing heat and pain. She cried out and Aziz stopped moving. Tasira pulled his face down and kissed him. She looked at his face and saw the worry.

"It is alright, Aziz. This is to be expected." Tasira prepared herself more pain until she felt something move on her chest and was amazed as she looked down.

Aziz also watched as the medallion he wore moved. The female medallion raised up off of Tasira's breasts, and as they touched, a bright golden glow, like the twin suns of Tuulani, enveloped the lovers. Tasira felt the pain disappear and a heat inside her beginning to grow. Aziz raised his head as the pleasure inside of him intensified.

They made love that night and when they finished, the medallions gently returned to their owners. The couple lay in the bed together on the edge of sleep.

"I love you, Aziz," Tasira whispered as she fell to sleep. The large Xoran who had spent so many years alone had tears running down his face as he moved Tasira closer to him and felt her snuggle into his embrace. He could hear her rhythmic breathing as she drifted off to sleep.

"I love you, too, Tasira," Aziz whispered softly as he covered them both with a light blanket. "I will love you forever," he said as he gently kissed the top of her head.

Chapter Thirty-Eight

The next morning, Aziz woke to an empty bed. He was worried as he got up to dress. He found a note on top of his neatly folded clothes.

Aziz,

I am sorry to leave you this morning, but Seta asked me to meet her in the library before we were bonded last night. I will find you after the meeting is concluded.

Love,

Tasira

Aziz was relieved that she had written a note, but was a little frustrated that he could not awaken with Tasira in his arms. He wondered what was so important that she would leave this morning. Seta must have had a good reason, he thought to himself as he dressed.

Seta was waiting for Tasira as she sipped on her morning tea. She did not wait long though, Tasira was a woman who kept her word.

"Good morning, Seta!"

"Good Morning, Tasira. It appears that you survived the night and are happy," Seta said in dry humor as she looked at the young woman's happy face.

"Would you like a cup of tea?" Tasira nodded and Seta poured another cup. "I am sorry to have taken you away from Aziz, but one of the Elders asked if we could meet him here. I don't know what this is about, but as I said before, Lyn does not do anything without a reason."

"Lyn?" Tasira asked, confused. "Wasn't he the one that asked me if I was truly from the city? Seta nodded and was about to say something, when a deep male voice sounded behind Tasira.

"I see that you two are ready for this meeting." Lyn smiled a little and then became serious again. "Please follow me into the library," he motioned as he walked away.

The few minutes it took to get to the library seemed to take hours. Soon enough though, the three of them entered the cramped quarters of the small library.

"This is something we have waited for generations to happen." Lyn looked at the two young women and then reached inside his pocket. He pulled out two jewels and looked at them very closely. One was a glowing burgundy and the other was bright silver. Neither had ever seen jewels like this before. These were not the typical book jewels they were used to viewing.

Lyn took the burgundy jewel and moved between Tasira and Seta. The jewel glowed brighter when it was in front of Tasira. He performed the same ritual with the shining silver stone. The silver stone shone like a star as it reached Seta. He placed the burgundy stone in Tasira's hand and gave the silver stone to Seta. He smiled at them and turned around to retrieve a small box.

Inside the box was a round, hollow piece of the same black metal that comprised Mara's ring. The metal seemed to be in constant motion but still stayed in the same shape.

Lyn placed the metal tube over a round engraving in the library wall. The metal fit slipped past the edges of the engraving and fit like a key in a lock. The wall began to move a little, revealing a doorway. As it opened, a room behind the library began to emerge.

The room was covered in jewels that lit up as Seta and Tasira passed through the doorway. As large as the space was, no one would've never known it was there. It was completely hidden.

Lyn directed to the two females to move toward the other side of the room. There, next to one another were two small altars. The altars had holes in the center which appeared to be made for the jewels that Seta and Tasira held.

"You must find out which stone correctly fits in the resting place of the altars. This must be done correctly the first time or our chance will have been wasted." Lyn looked at the two of them, "You must devise a way to decide. We have no knowledge of how to complete the ceremony. I'm sorry, but the burden falls upon your shoulders."

Tasira and Seta clasped hands. "We will do this together, Seta, " Tasira smiled.

As they walked closer to the altars, they nodded to one another and placed the jewels in their correct places. As they did, there were two bright flashes of light, one on each of the women. Tasira and Seta collapsed on the floor, unconscious.

"Seta! Tasira! Please wake up!" Lyn yelled and shook them. He was confused, he hadn't seen what had happened. They were still breathing but neither one would respond. Lyn ran out to get help and saw the men sitting at the table for the morning meal.

"Come quickly!" Lyn yelled. "I need your help!"

The men who were eating, turned around and looked at the Elder. Aziz had a bad feeling in the pit of his stomach.

"Help you with what?" Aziz quickly got up from the bench where he sat and ran over to the old male.

"It is Seta and Tasira. They are laying on the floor in the library chamber and I cannot awaken them!" Lyn yelled as he turned around to lead the now scurrying men toward the library. Aziz ran full speed and was there long before the rest of the men.

"Tasira! Seta!" Aziz yelled at the two women. He scooped them up, one in each arm and carried them out into the sun. He handed Seta to one of the other men, Tul. Then he sat down on the ground with Tasira.

"Tasira, wake up! Please wake up!" Aziz chanted over and over. He sat there for most of the morning with Tasira until Dela came up to him.

"Aziz, take your wife into your chamber! She cannot be in the sun as long as you!" Dela scolded. "You will be able to take care of her better in your room." Aziz dropped his head.

"Dela?" Aziz looked up at the old woman. Dela gave him a stern look.

"Aziz, if you don't take your wife and put her in your bed, I will never speak to you again. Tasira is a strong woman. Look at her, she still breathes and I am sure that she will come back to you!" Dela finished.

"Now...stop feeling sorry for yourself and take your mate home!" she yelled. Everyone within listening distance stopped and looked at Dela. She had done more talking in the last few days than they had heard in years. Even before her mate had died, they had never heard her raise her voice. There must be something special about these two that would bring out such emotion from her. When Dela looked around, everyone pretended that they had not heard anything. Dela gave a sharp nod and walked away.

Chapter Thirty-Nine

"So, your plan is to just sit there and do nothing!" D'kal raged at her husband. "Qata hasn't come to speak to me in over a week, that little bitch! She cannot ignore me and expect no consequences." D'kal reached for the slim cane that she had used to beat Qata before. Tavon raised his eyebrows.

"Do you think you can just walk into the House of Nathan, beat the child and then walk back here? Are you insane?" Tavon walked up to D'kal and grabbed the cane from her hand.

"Perhaps I should use this to beat some sense into you," he looked at her coldly. "Leave her alone. After I become the Ra Shan, you can do what you wish. I don't expect that I will have much say in the matter anyway." Tavon threw the cane into the corner as he walked out of the room.

D'kal watched him leave the room and then went and picked up the cane. She absently caressed the cane as she thought about what Tavon had said to her. He was right, she couldn't just walk into that house and beat the child. But she wasn't ready to give the girl her freedom either. She paid for that little whore and she was going to get her money's worth one way or another.

D'kal had a thought, and it brought an evil smile to her face. She slapped the cane lightly in her hand. Oh yes, this was definitely a good plan.

Nathan and Mara were lying in bed. They had no reason to rush to the Great Room. Something had changed in Mara when she had arrived and now, with Tasira declared dead, he would have expected her to fall deeper into depression.

But in the last three days, oddly enough, she was beginning to come back to be the Mara he had known when he met her. This morning had shown him that she could still convince him to stay in bed.

"Nathan, I will be in the practice room with Tamara if you need me." Mara saw Nathan's eyebrows shoot up. "I know I have been a little off since we came to Tuulani, but something has changed in me. I feel like I did before we came here. It was the oddest feeling." Mara paused as she tried to explain.

"It was as if the part of me that had been removed was returned a couple of days ago." She looked at Nathan as she dressed in her practice uniform. She was pulling on her boots when she realized the coincidence.

"That's when we finished the mourning for Tasira. I wonder if the Elders put the request in the official record. We never got a chance to ask them with all of Nathaniel and Qata's issues." She smiled at Nathan. "They both look so happy. I am glad we will have her as a member of our family." Nathan watched Mara as she quietly slipped past the door and went down the hall. She was the most amazing woman he had ever met. She was his perfect match.

Hours after Mara had finished her exercises, there was a loud knock on the front door. Nathan motioned for Qata, Nathaniel and the others to go into the Great Hall. Caleb ushered the curious youngsters into the large room and closed the doors. After Nathan was sure that everyone was out of harm's way, he opened the outside door. It was Tavon.

"Tavon, there is nothing we can do until the Elders reach their decision." Nathan looked the older male in the eyes, "And make no mistake, we will fight you at every turn. You and I both know that Qata is not being held against her will." Nathan finished in a threatening tone. Tavon held up his hand, in a placating manner.

"Now, now Nathan. There is no need to be inhospitable." Tavon smiled as he reached into his coat pocket and pulled out a document.

"I come bearing gifts and peace. I do not want to have a fight with you. In fact, this is quite the opposite," he smiled as he handed the official document to Nathan. Nathan read it and looked up at Tavon.

"You want Qata and Nathaniel to be bonded?" Nathan looked at the other male suspiciously. "How did you go from accusing us of kidnapping Qata to wanting her bonded with Nathaniel?"

Qata and Mara stood at the doors and listened to the conversation. Qata's eyes flew open when she heard what Nathan had said. Mara shook her head no and motioned for her to not speak. Tamara was retrieving her practice staff in case this was only a ruse to get her father to open the door, so others could rush in and take Qata. Mara looked back at Tamara and motioned for her to bring her practice staff too. Tavon looked at Nathan with a feigned wounded look.

"Well, you see, my wife was just concerned that her adopted daughter was being harmed. I have spoken to her about this and we agree that if Qata truly loves your

Nathaniel, well then, who are we to stand in their way? D'kal and I just want to have the bonding ceremony in the Hall of Elders. We want it to be a city-wide event with parties and laughter ringing through every citizen's home." Tavon smiled at Nathan widely.

"Come with me to the Hall of Elders now and put your seal on the bonding document. They will put it in the official record and we can set a date. What do you say, Nathan? Shall we stop this fight between us?" Nathan looked at the document and then back up at Tavon.

"Alright, I will get my seal and we will go to the Hall of Elders. We will stop this rivalry right now and we will let the city and the Hall of Elders decide who will be Ra Shan. This bonding has nothing to do with politics, it is about love," Nathan finished and went to his study to get the ring that represented the House of Nathan. Tavon and Nathan left together and walked to the Hall of Elders to present the document.

D'kal sat at home with Foro wondering how well her husband was doing with Nathan. She told him to be very careful, Nathan was much smarter that he was given credit for in this house. D'kal assumed that Mara had the same hold over her husband.

Mara was a tricky one and even for her size, she could fight most anyone D'kal supposed. She had certainly got her hits in with D'kal that afternoon so long ago.

"Perhaps I will have a second chance to kill you after all, Mara," D'kal smiled.

Chapter Forty

The Hall of Elders foyer was vacant except for Nathan and Tavon. The two men sat on opposite sides of the room until they were called in to speak to the Elders. Jes raised his eyebrows when he saw the two men walk in together. He looked both men in the eyes and could see that Nathan was as suspicious as he was of this turn of events.

"You have asked for our counsel?" Jes asked in a monotone voice. Tavon looked at the Elders and smiled.

"Yes, this will be a glorious event if we have the blessing of the Elders," Tavon said in an overly happy voice. It reminded Jes of oil spilling over his fingers. It was smooth and yet left you feeling as if you needed to wash yourself clean.

Tavon handed over the bonding document to Jes. "So, you wish for Qata to bond with Nathaniel?" Jes asked in a surprised voice.

"Oh yes, we want our little girl to be happy. It seems that this is what she wants. So D'kal and I have decided to let her make her own decision," Tavon finished. Jes looked at Nathan.

"I see that you have not yet put your seal on this document. Are you not agreeable to this bonding?" Jes asked. Nathan shook his head.

"No, I just wanted to wait until the Elders had viewed the document and had approved it. My son, Nathaniel has wanted to bond with Qata for a very long time now. I will be relieved to see him get his chance at happiness." Nathan finished, giving a meaningful look to Jes. Jes nodded.

Nathan was quite the sly one. He knew that if the Elders gave their blessing before he put his seal on the document, any breach of the terms of the document would be held as a high offense. There were serious punishments for not upholding the law of the Elders. Nathan knew the Elders would support the bonding, thereby putting pressure on Tavon and his family to comply.

"Well then, Nathan, I would ask if you would put your seal on the document also." Jes smiled as Nathan walked up and placed his seal on the paper. Jes smiled, nodded to Nathan and then to Tavon.

"We will have the ceremony in two weeks, when the suns are setting on the horizon." Both Tavon and Nathan nodded in agreement. Nathan was preparing to leave when Tavon started speaking again.

"Now, about the day of the event. I would like the entire city to have parties the day before through the day after the bonding," Tavon smiled. He looked at Nathan, "All at my expense, of course, Nathan. I know you do not own as much as I do, so let the parties be my present to both of our families." Nathan smiled stiffly at Tavon.

"I will contribute as well, Tavon." Nathan looked up at the Elders and the specifically at Jes. "We will let you decide what the parties will be, and what each of our families should do to prepare." Jes nodded.

"Alright Nathan, Tavon, I will make you both a list of things you will contribute. That will give us a neutral, third-party plan to allow the preparation for each day's events." Jes stopped and wrote a list of things on two pieces of paper. The first one was given to Tavon, the second to Nathan.

Both men opened their folded notes and read them. Tavon carefully folded his and put it in his pocket. Nathan nodded and folded his in the same way. The two men looked at one another and then went home. Jes shook his head and spoke to the other Elders.

"This may be a catastrophic day for the city. I fear there is much more to plan than parties before that day arrives." They all nodded and then went to the back chamber to discuss and plan for the bonding ceremony.

Nathan arrived back at his home about an hour after he had left. Mara was glad to see him coming home safe and ran up to Nathan and threw her arms as far as they could go around him. She looked up at him and then took a step backwards. There was a seriousness about his look that worried her.

"Nathan, what is wrong?" Mara asked as she looked at him. She was wary about the news before, and now she knew that all was not what it seemed.

"We must prepare for the Elders. They are visiting us tonight after the suns have set." Nathan motioned for Mara and the other adults to meet with him in the Great Hall. Nathan asked Caleb if he would make sure that the children, including Nathaniel and Qata were in another room and not listening.

"What has happened Nathan?" Ket, his grandfather asked when they were all seated at the table. The others waited in terse anticipation.

"Tavon has agreed to let Qata bond with Nathaniel. But he wouldn't do this unless there was some advantage for him and D'kal." Nathan placed his hands on the table.

"He has asked for three days of parties to be held the day before, the day of, and the day after the bonding ceremony." No one at the table spoke, but they were all thinking the same thing. Something terrible was being planned for those three days. Nathan raised his eyebrows, nodded, and continued.

"The Elders blessed the bonding before I put our seal on it. By law, there are serious penalties for interrupting an event that has the blessing of the Elders." Nathan looked around. "Tavon was almost giddy when I put my seal on the document. This has me worried." Nathan looked down and thought.

"I do not understand," Mara looked confused. "If Tavon has put his seal on the document, doesn't he have to obey the blessing of the Elders." Nathan nodded. Ket looked up with his eyes wide.

"They are not worried about the Elders, Mara." Ket looked at her. "They wouldn't have to worry if they forced us to bow out of the ceremony." Nathan looked up at Ket.

"Or worse yet, they wouldn't have to worry if the Elders were no longer in control of the city." Nathan finished. Mara shook her head.

"They wouldn't dare!" Mara said outraged. It took Mara only a couple of seconds to follow what Nathan was implying. As the realization hit her, her face became pale.

"They are going to bring in their supporters and try to kill us and the Elders, aren't they? They would have all of the power D'kal could ever want." She finished in a quieter tone. Nathan nodded.

"This is the 'list' of party items that our house is to bring. Jes gave it to me himself." On the top of the paper were inane things such as type of food and how many baskets of it were required. On the bottom of the list was a sentence, *"They will try to kill all of us. The other Elders and I will visit your home tonight. Nod your head if you understand."*

"I will go and prepare something for the Elders to eat and drink. Caleb is busy watching the children," Ket got up and went to the kitchen to prepare for the Elders arrival.

"Should we tell Qata and Nathaniel?" Nathan asked Mara. She shook her head.

"No. They do not have the experience that we do in dealing with these kinds of situations. They are too honest and I do not think that we should count on them to be able to act as if they are unaware of the danger." Mara looked at Nathan, "If D'kal or any of her followers touch my child or his beloved, I will kill her." Nathan grabbed her and shook her a little.

"You cannot let your feelings show, Mara. If we are to protect those we love, we must stay calm." Nathan reminded her. She nodded and looked at him with a steely gaze.

"I can play the game very well my love. Or have you forgotten the hell I survived on Earth?" Mara looked at him with a determined look. "I will be calm, and you know I can hide my feelings when necessary. I will even lie if I have no other option." She looked at the floor in an effort to center herself.

"I will say it again. If D'kal touches me or my loved ones, I will kill her. Do you understand me?" She looked at Nathan and he nodded. This was the woman who saved him and the others from the genocide against the Tuulans. Mara had stood against those of her own species to do what was right. She had always fulfilled her promises, and he almost felt sorry for the House of Tavon. *Almost.*

Chapter Forty-One

It had been three days and Tasira had not awakened. Aziz had tended to Tasira every moment he was awake. Dela came in and tended to the young woman when Aziz would pass out from worry and exhaustion. He had only succumbed to sleep once during Tasira's second day, and since then he had been by her side every moment.

Aziz laid next to her and watched her breathe. The rhythm of it was hypnotic and it kept Aziz's attention. He had never asked the Priestess for anything but a woman to love.

The Priestess wouldn't be so cruel as to take her the day after he had bonded with her. He caressed Tasira's arm and put her hand inside his. He remembered the day she grabbed his hand for no reason and how surprised he had been that she was not afraid of him.

He decided to pray to the Priestess once more. He held Tasira's hand between his palms.

"Please Priestess, do not take her from me. Show her the way back to me. Please."

Aziz closed his eyes and held her hand tight. Tasira's ze'ev, Tinku was laying on the other side of her and whined. He missed her too. Dela saw them from the doorway and shook her head silently. They should have been given more time together than they had. Dela looked at the young female once more and noticed that there was a bulge under the blanket that they had covered her with that morning. She walked over to Tasira and pulled back the covers and was amazed. It was the woman's medallion. And it was glowing.

"Aziz," Dela whispered. "Aziz!" She whispered louder this time and nudged the big male's shoulder. Aziz was not in the mood for another 'talk' from Dela and refused to open his eyes.

"What!" Aziz whispered back. "Can't you leave us alone? No matter what you tell me, it is not going to bring her back!" He further turned his back toward the old woman in anger. Dela was annoyed now. She smacked the back of his head.

"If you don't want to listen to me, then open your eyes and look for yourself!" Dela whispered loudly back at Aziz.

Aziz opened his eyes and saw the glow of the medallion. He placed his hand over it and it grew brighter. He was amazed and looked at Dela. She was standing, her arms crossed over her chest in an "I told you so" stance. Dela snorted at him and then walked into the other room.

In the other bedroom, Tul had been taking care of Seta. No one had known that the two had been having a romance for quite a while. No one except Dela. She saw everything and said nothing. Unless it was necessary.

Apparently, Tul had asked Seta to bond with him, but she had declined. Still, Tul made sure that Seta was well cared for. It was obvious to Dela that Tul loved Seta deeply.

Dela walked into the room and noticed that Seta had a woman's medallion around her neck and that it was also glowing. It was a sign from above. She walked over to the sleeping Tul and nudged him awake.

"We must put the two women together." Dela ordered. Tul looked at her as if she had lost her mind. Dela crossed her arms and looked at Tul.

"Now!" she yelled, "Not later!" The woman's voice boomed throughout the Hall. "Now!" Tul got up quickly and carried Seta into Tasira's room. He looked at Aziz and motioned behind him at Dela.

"She thinks this is the best thing for both women," Tul shrugged and laid Seta next to Tasira. The two men watched as the glowing medallions got brighter.

"Pull back the covers, Aziz, and let us see what happens." Dela suggested. Aziz nodded, carefully pulled back the blanket, and moved Tasira so that she and Seta were touching. From the moment that the two women touched, the medallions glowed as bright as daylight and rose off their chests until they were hovering over the women. The medallions moved toward each other, touched with a slight metallic sound, and then slowly laid back down on their chests.

Within moments, the women awakened and looked around. They were amazed to be back in Tasira's room and laying together.

Tasira looked at Aziz, "How long have I been asleep?" she asked her husband. She felt refreshed, as though she had taken a long nap. Aziz leaned over her and grabbed her up in his arms.

"This is the third day, Tasira." He held her tightly and smiled as he slowly twirled around. "I would have waited by your side forever if that is what was needed," he twirled her around again.

"Tul, you have waited for me?" Seta asked the man who stood by her side. She got up from the bed and put her arms around his neck. "Thank you, Tul, for taking care of me." Seta kissed him and he pulled her closer to his body, wanting to feel all of her, until he remembered their agreement. He gently pushed her back from him and smiled flatly.

"I am glad that you have awakened as well, Seta." Tul stated in a reserved voice. He knew that Seta did not love him as he loved her. He was glad that she was back, but he held no hopes about a future with Seta.

Seta looked at Tul and sighed. She had never led him to believe that they would have anything other than the relationship that they had now. She would rather have nothing more than an errant kiss once in a while. When her last mate died, she vowed to never go through that pain again.

She was saddened when Tul left the room, but it was for the best. Better to have him angry, than to expect more and have his heart broken. Dela watched Tul leave and sighed heavily. She didn't like the sadness he carried now, but Seta was right to not let him think that there would be more.

Seta looked at Tasira and Aziz. She was happy for them and she knew that they were a good match. Aziz, the Xoran. The warrior with the soft heart. And Tasira, the small, soft young Tuulan with the heart of a warrior. They were perfect for one another. Seta walked out of the room and left them to their privacy.

Chapter Forty-Two

The next morning, Aziz awoke and was afraid to open his eyes. What if all of the happenings were only a dream and Tasira was not there. What if she was next to him and had never awakened. He would wait a while before ruining this moment.

"Aziz. I know that you are awake, you can't fool me!" Tasira giggled at her husband trying to pretend that he was still asleep. Aziz's eyes flew open and he rolled onto his side to look at her.

"I was afraid to open my eyes. I did not know if what happened last evening was real. I was afraid you would still be unconscious and that I had dreamed everything." Aziz looked at her and touched her silky black hair. She had told him that it was the same as her mother's hair and her green eyes were from her mother as well. Her father must consider himself fortunate. He knew that he did.

"Well, last night was no dream. We were awake for most of the night and I remember it very well." Tasira smiled as she teased him.

"We should get up and have something to eat. I'm starving," she said in a happy voice. Aziz watched her get up from the bed and wash herself in the basin. She put on the blue dress that Dela had given to her. She looked beautiful. She looked back and threw the wet washcloth at him. "Are you joining me for breakfast, sleepyhead?" Aziz felt the washcloth hit his cheek and smiled.

"Sleepyhead? I will show you who you are dealing with, Tasira!" Aziz got up from the bed and chased her, playfully around the room. She was considerably smaller, so she could slip around furniture easier and run across the bed. Eventually though, he caught up with her and swung her up in his arms. Tasira squealed with delight and started laughing.

"Alright, I give up Aziz! You win!" She squealed and laughed again as he nibbled on her neck. Seta heard the play and the laughter in Tasira's bedroom. She was loathe to stop them, but she knew that she and Tasira needed to be prepared for the next part of their journey together. Seta knocked and the play on the other side of the door stopped.

"Yes?" Tasira answered.

"I hate to bother you, but we must go back to the chamber," Seta said in a sympathetic voice. The door flung open and there stood Aziz, completely naked.

"Tasira will never be going back to that place! Is it not enough that I almost lost her once?" The big man stood in front of Seta, his chest heaving with anger as he breathed. "No. She is not going. I will not have it," he finished and slammed the door shut in Seta's face.

Seta smiled, shook her head, and waited a few minutes longer. She was leaning against the wall and could hear the argument progress in the bedroom. She folded her arms over her chest and moved to rest against the wall on the opposite side of the hallway. She knew it wouldn't take too long.

The door opened again. This time it was Tasira. She looked at Seta and nodded and walked to the library's hidden chamber. Seta followed with a smile on her face. This small woman was not one to start a fight, but she certainly knew how to win one.

THE REVELATIONS OF TUULANI

Chapter Forty-Three

The two women walked into the small library. Seta retrieved the key to the chamber and looked over at Tasira. Tasira placed her hand over Seta's and they opened the doorway together. They closed the doorway when they had reached the other side. They would have no interruptions.

The chamber lit up with the glow of the jewels on each side of the room. Seta and Tasira knew instinctively what jewels they need to take first.

Seta, who had been chosen by the silver jewel, would view all of the books on her side of the library which were colored in varied blues, whites, grays and iridescent clear.

Tasira would view the varied orange, red, yellow and pink hues. Each woman would have their own separate knowledge, but together they would posses all of the secrets of Tuulani.

Tasira and Seta chose five stones and sat down to view them. Seta sat at the silver stone's altar and Tasira sat at the burgundy stone's altar. They looked at each other as they placed their first book in the viewer. A rush of information was transported into their minds and within minutes the book was completed. The ritual was performed until each woman had viewed over a hundred books.

Tasira looked at Seta, "How long have we been in here?" Seta looked up and closed her eyes.

"It is time for the evening meal. We should go back and be with the others." Seta finished and Tasira nodded. They walked out together and the door closed behind them automatically. The women looked at each other, smiled, and continued on their way to the evening meal.

As Tasira and Seta entered the Great Hall, the conversation stopped. The citizens of the town paused and watched them sit down at the head of the table, together. Aziz was already sitting just off to Tasira's right and Dela sat to Seta's left. Tul was sitting by another female and it was clear that he was turning his attentions to her. Seta was glad for Tul and smiled at him and nodded. He smiled back and then began the conversation with his companion once more.

Aziz looked at Tasira and saw that there was a change in her. She looked as if she had matured mentally in the last few hours. She and Seta both looked different in appearance then they had before. Perhaps different was not the right word.

They looked *more*. Aziz was not sure what that meant, but he would attempt to understand it. He would investigate further as best he could. Later.

The evening meal was filled with conversations and laughter, but Tasira could hardly wait to go home with Aziz. She looked at him and smiled. He reached for her hand and gave it a tight squeeze. Tasira was so happy that she could barely contain it. Moments later, Seta stood up and got the attention of everyone in the village.

"Tasira and I have only five more cycles of the suns before we must go to the city." Seta looked at everyone and then turned her gaze at Tasira and Aziz.

"Tasira and I will not return to this place. Anyone who wishes to come with us can do so, but if you decide to stay behind, we will not stop you." Seta looked at her plate.

"Once we leave this place, the natak we will use will not work again. It will shut down forever and you will not be able to follow us. That is, unless you follow the quest that Tasira took when she came to us here." Seta looked at the faces around the table once more.

"You will have five more days to make your decision. We will let you know when it is time." With that said, Seta got up from the table and walked into her room. As Seta closed the door, Aziz took Tasira's hand and walked with her to their bedroom.

"Did you know of the move to the city before Seta announced it tonight?" Aziz asked. Tasira shook her head.

"No Aziz, I did not." Tasira looked at her mate and continued. "Each of us has our own knowledge. I have mine and Seta has hers. The sacred books decide which one of us gets to read their knowledge. There are things that I will know that Seta will not. We will only be able to access that knowledge when it is needed." She looked at Aziz and stroked the side of his cheek. "Do you understand what I mean?" Aziz shook his head.

"Not exactly...but as long as you remain my mate, it will not matter." Aziz smiled and Tasira smiled back. She had seen that smile before and it beguiled her. She knew that she would be getting less sleep than she had planned.

Chapter Forty-Four

"Nathan? Where are you?" Mara called out for her husband. "I am in the bedroom, Mara," Nathan answered. Mara went up to their room and there was Nathan, trying to finish getting dressed. He was having difficulty with his jacket buttons. His large fingers could not get one buttoned without unbuttoning the others. He was frustrated at his limitations. Mara smiled and shook her head.

"You could have just called for me. " Mara looked up at her husband and smiled.

"I can help you get *dressed* once in a while, too." She winked at him and he smiled back. It was good to have the Mara he knew back again. He just wished he would've been able to have his whole family together for Nathaniel's bonding ceremony.

Tasira would have been so happy for her brother. Nathan shook his head slightly to get that thought out of his head. Today was going to be difficult enough without adding those thoughts to the problem. Mara finished buttoning his jacket for him.

"There! Now if you need anything else, just call for me!" Mara smiled and patted his bottom as she walked into the hallway. She was a vision of beauty today. She had purchased some cloth from another citizen and had sewn a long, blue dress for the occasion. Under the skirt she would have her knife and her black uniform pants, rolled up so they could not be seen. If there was any trouble today, she would tear away the skirt and be ready for battle. She was perfect. Beautiful and deadly to anyone who threatened her loved ones.

Nathaniel was also nervous, but it had nothing to do with the trouble his parents were anticipating today. They hadn't told him, Qata, or the twins anything about it. He was just nervous about the ceremony. He didn't hear his mother walk into his room.

"Nathaniel, can I help you with anything?" Mara asked softly.

"Mother! You startled me!" Nathaniel said in a somewhat harsh tone. Moments later, he realized how he must have sounded. "I'm sorry mother. I am just so nervous." Mara nodded.

"I know that this is a big step for a young man and woman. I am just happy that she was able to consent to the bonding before it happened," she laughed a little. "Your father used the medallion on me and thought that I hated him for not getting my consent." Mara smiled. "At least you won't have that problem with Qata." Mara went over and hugged her son. "Everything will be just fine. You'll see," Mara finished as she walked out the door. She prayed she wasn't telling her son a lie.

The last door Mara stopped at was Qata's. She peeked through the doorway and saw her soon-to-be new family member. She was beautiful in the dress D'kal had sent over to her. When it arrived, the dress was inspected by the Elders of the house and she and Nathan as well. It appeared to be a dress and nothing more. They hung it in Qata's room and there it stayed until this morning.

"I see you have the dress on, Qata." Mara said. "It is just a couple of hours before you will be Nathaniel's mate and he yours."

Qata looked at Mara and blushed a little, "I know that I am probably not the ideal woman for your son, in your eyes. There have been things..." Mara interrupted her.

"What is in your past should remain in your past. As long as you and Nathaniel are happy, life will seem sweeter. That is all a mother wants. You will see when you have your own babes. All you want for them is to be happy." Mara went over and hugged the young woman.

"I'm glad that Nathaniel has found someone to love. Love him every day as if it is your last and your bonding will be joyful." Mara smiled again, "Call for me if you need anything." Mara made her way through the house and checked on everyone to make sure that all was ready.

D'kal was so excited that she was bouncing up and down on her toes. "It is almost time, Tavon. When the day is over, there will be nothing but prosperity for the House of Tavon. We will rule the city and the whole planet of Tuulani." She looked over to see her husband reading an old book.

"Are you listening to what I am saying, Tavon? Or are you too mesmerized by the book you are reading," she finished tersely. Tavon continued to look at the book.

"Do you know that there has never been a Kuutaran in our family before? We have always chosen other races to bond with." He looked at his wife. "I imagine that was because my ancestors knew that Kuutarans were a ruthless and self-serving bunch of thieves." Tavon looked at D'kal. "And I mean that in the most flattering way possible." Tavon looked at her with disgust, hidden by a smile.

"Why, if it weren't for you, I would have been happy to live out my miserable life alone." Tavon rose and took off his reading glasses.

"I just hope that today will fulfill your lust for vengeance and power." The anger in D'kal's gut burned as she watched her husband. He looked over at her as he set down his glass and walked past her.

"Now, now, my dear. You'll just have to wait until after the ceremony to arrange an accident for me." Tavon spoke over his shoulder. "Do make it a spectacular one, won't you?"

Chapter Forty-Five

With the last of the books read, Seta and Tasira readied their friends and families to go with them to the city. Dela, Tul and some of the others had decided to stay at the village. The city was not for them and they told Tasira that they would not be comfortable living with so many others.

Tasira gave them her blessing and completed the tasks she needed to before leaving. She walked into the bedroom where Aziz was gathering things to carry through the natak. Tasira laughed a little and Aziz looked up at her.

"What," Aziz asked as she entered the room. Tasira looked at the collection of bags hanging off his arms. She smiled at him again.

"We don't need to take everything, Aziz." She went over and helped him set the bags on the floor. "My family lives in the city and we will be able to live with them. They have a house with an entire wing that they do not use." She looked at him.

"Now let's decide together, what do we really need and what do we think we need? OK?" Aziz nodded his head and wondered if he would be able to like the city as much as Tasira did. He had his doubts, but he would live anywhere as long as she was with him.

A couple of hours later, Seta knocked on the door.

"It is time to leave, Tasira," she said in quiet, authoritative voice. Tasira nodded and Aziz picked up the three bags that they had packed. It had been quite the fight to get Aziz to believe her that they didn't need their cups or pans. Finally, though, she convinced him that the city would have everything they would need and that they only needed to bring their most personal items. The items they would truly miss.

Tasira, Aziz, Seta and about fifty others grouped together at the edge of Mabray. There were excited conversations and tearful goodbyes, but the group was now ready. Tasira looked back at the small group that decided to stay. Dela, Tul, Tul's soon-to-be wife, Su'na, and about ten others.

It had come down to two reasons. They couldn't bear to leave the life they had always known, or they were afraid of the people in the city making fun of them.

Some of those remaining had been born with the same conditions as the babies that had been born so many centuries ago. The medallion could have healed them, but they had decided to stay as they had been born. They would not bond with another and have their child born to carry the affliction further. So, they stayed, knowing that their family blood would end with them.

Tasira waved at them, tears falling down her face when they waved back for the last time. She turned around and put her hand with Seta's on the natak.

"Ke hirsa te ke ka hirsa altan. Ka hirsa se te bakt la hirsa altan la'alam," The two women chanted over and over. Soon a bright light appeared as a small point and then widened to reveal the city that they longed to go to. They would appear in front of the sand wall and then use the key Seta held to open the gateway. All they had to do was take that first step. Tasira led the group.

"Follow me. I have gone through a natak before. It was how I got from Earth to Tuulani. There is nothing to fear, it is the same as moving from one room to another," Tasira urged the group to follow. She stepped through and stood on the other side, motioning for them to follow quickly.

Seta was next, with Aziz right behind her. The remaining fifty quickly moved through the doorway and into the blistering hot of the desert. The doorway closed behind them with a blink. The village was now gone and to return would mean weeks of travel through the desert. They had to go the rest of the way with Seta and Tasira now.

Seta took the key out of her pocket. It was the first thing that the books had shown to her. The key had been hidden when the old male had known he was going to die. He put its location and the instruction on how to use the key, in the last book Seta read. She held the key in her hand, it was tarnished and well worn and was only about the size of one of Tasira's fingers. It looked very small in Seta's hand, but she said the words to open the archway. *"Br'ra natak ha'a. Br'ra natak ha'a."* Seta chanted over and over.

It was over an hour later and the archway had not opened. The people who had followed Seat and Tasira were suffering in the blazing heat of the suns. They had not taken much water with them. They thought it would be a short step through the natak and then through the archway. They had not prepared for this. Tasira walked over to Seta who was sitting dejectedly on the hot sand. She looked at the key and then squeezed it hard in her hand. The key shattered under the pressure. It was too old and fragile to be of any use. It had been assumed that the key would be found hundreds of years ago. Tasira looked at the rubble of the shattered key in Seta's hand, then she looked at Seta.

"Get up." Tasira ordered as she held out her hand to Seta. Seta nodded and accepted the help from her friend.

"Seta, I need you to calm the others, they are scared," Tasira looked at her friend. "I am going to ask Aziz to help me contact the visage of the Priestess Batah." Seta looked at her strangely.

"The Priestess Batah died millennia ago. What is this visage you will talk to?" Seta asked. Tasira looked at her friend and could see that she was afraid, too.

"You need to trust me, OK?" Tasira said gently. Seta nodded and moved over to the others to try to calm them. Tasira walked over to Aziz.

"Will you help me contact Batah?" Tasira looked at her husband. He smiled up at her and got up from the sand.

"Anything, Tasira. I will help you," he smiled and then looked at her with a wrinkled brow. "I don't know anything about contacting Batah." Tasira smiled back at him.

"Reach as high as you can with your hands, Aziz." He did as Tasira asked and she stepped back to take a look at how tall he could reach. She nodded.

"Alright Aziz, now can you do that while I stand on the flat part of your hands?" Aziz nodded.

"Of course, I can. You are so very light that I could stand there as long as you needed," he said to her as he boasted a little. He smiled at her and winked. Tasira winked back.

"Then let's try it," she challenged. Aziz smiled and lifted his wife up with his hands. He let go of one ankle and bent his hand back so she could stand on it. With that completed, he did the same with the other hand. Tasira was standing on top of his hands and could see over the wall of sand. She lifted her hands in the air and closed her eyes.

"*Ke te su'un Batah? Ke te su'un Batah?*" Tasira chanted skyward. She kept chanting until someone yelled, 'There is a doorway opening!' Tasira opened her eyes and Aziz moved his hands and caught her in his arms. She kissed him and then got down to walk through the door. Seta motioned to Tasira to go first. Tasira nodded and walked toward her friend Batah.

"If I could hug you Batah, I would." Tasira smiled at the hologram.

"I wish you could too Tasira. But there is no time to waste, there is much you need to know. May I update you, Tasira?" Tasira nodded and Batah placed each one of her hands on Tasira's temples. A light glowed between her hands and Tasira's temples and Tasira closed her eyes at the pain. Aziz was about to step in, but the ordeal was over in a flash. He caught Tasira in his arms as she shook off the nausea that always came with Batah's touch. Tasira looked at Aziz.

"I need you to carry me to my father's house. I need to get to my family fast and I am still a little unsteady. Will you do that for me?" Aziz nodded.

"Tell me where your home is and I will bring you there, Tasira." Aziz looked down at his wife. She was so little and carried so much responsibility. He wished that there was more he could do for her. He yelled at the others to follow him and soon Seta was running closely behind Aziz. Tasira told Aziz where to turn and soon they were standing at the front door of the House of Nathan. Aziz set Tasira down on her feet and watched as his wife ran through the door, yelling for her family.

"Is anyone here?" Tasira yelling as the tears fell down her face. "Please someone, answer me!" Tasira fell to her knees, realizing she had failed. If what Batah had showed her was true, she had failed and her family was going to die. She heard the sound of footsteps beside her, "Aziz, I have failed. They aren't here."

Chapter Forty-Six

"Tasira," an older voice asked, "Tasira, is that really you?" Tasira looked up and saw the faces of Pel and Caleb.

"Thank the Priestess that you are here," Tasira cried out. "Have my parents gone to the bonding ceremony?" she asked. The two old men were so shocked at seeing Tasira that they just nodded their heads.

"Is it being held at the Hall of Elders?" she asked. Again, they could only nod with their mouths slightly agape.

"OK!" Tasira turned around. "Aziz, we need to get to the Hall of Elders. My family will be murdered if we don't hurry! You must carry both me and Seta, can you do this," she implored with an anxious yet authoritative voice. Aziz nodded at Tasira and then smiled at the two men who were standing there, frozen, at the sight of his wife.

It was good to know that she had a way with all of those around her, not just him. He felt a little smug with himself as he scooped up the two women and ran for the Hall of Elders. The two older men had stayed home to watch the house. They looked at each other.

"Was that really Tasira?" Pel asked Caleb. Caleb nodded his head.

"Uh huh" he answered, unable to say more.

"Was that a…a Xoran male with her?" Pel asked.

"Uh huh," Caleb answered again.

"Let's go talk about this over a cup of tea," Pel suggested and Caleb nodded his head. He quietly followed Pel into the kitchen where they sat for a while and discussed what they had and had not seen.

Within a few minutes, Aziz reached the Hall of Elders. There were large Tuulan men guarding the doors. Supporters of the House of Tavon, Tasira surmised. Tasira told Aziz to wait for her behind one of the large statues that graced the center of the city. He started to disagree with Tasira, but she said that if she needed his help, he would know it. She needed him to be their surprise attack if necessary. Tasira kissed Aziz passionately, and then moved around the statue to walk up the front stairs.

"No one is allowed in the Hall of Elders," a big Tuulan male stepped forward. A weapon graced his hand and his hip. Tasira looked at him with a suggestive smile.

"I am surprised that you would need to bring a weapon to a bonding ceremony." Tasira cooed at him. "I would think you are weapon enough," she smiled. Aziz gnashed his teeth together. He had never felt this jealous before. Tasira should have told him her plan.

"What do you think, Seta, do any of these men need a weapon tonight?" Seta smiled at Tasira. She didn't know how Tasira learned to act this way, but she was definitely distracting the men.

"Oh, I don't think so Tasira. These men are over armed." Seta said in a hypnotic voice as she walked by each man and collected his sword, knife or other weapon they carried. She laid the weapons carefully in the fire burning in front of them. As soon as that was completed, Tasira nodded to Aziz.

"Aziz, will you make sure these men get what is coming to them?" Tasira winked at her husband. She placed a hand on her hip.

"Don't kill them, just make sure that they are unable to come in after us. OK?" Aziz smiled at his wife. Oh, he would definitely make sure that they would get what was coming to them.

Tasira could hear Aziz punching the men, violently, in front of the building. She counted nine as he knocked each one out. Nine. That was the same number as the Elders. Tasira put a hand over her mouth as she realized what that would mean. There would be no stopping Tavon and D'kal.

Seta and Tasira continued to walk through the foyer and then to the partially open door of the Hall. They could see that there were many people with weapons. It was only a matter of time before tragedy happened. Tasira spotted a woman pouring something in the punch.

So…if the blood bath didn't kill them, the poison would. Tasira could feel Seta grab her hand. Like magic, everyone in the room stopped moving. There was a strange stillness to the air. Seta let go of her hand and the others were talking as they had before. Tasira nodded in understanding and grabbed Seta's hand.

Time stopped for everyone but Tasira and Seta. They opened the door just enough to get inside the Hall. They carefully moved around the room and placed the weapons on the altar for everyone to see. Tasira tipped the punchbowl over and waited for the contents to spill over. Seta looked at her.

"The bowl will turn over and fall as soon as we let go of each other's hands. We must finish disarming the guests or we may have a war on our hands." Seta stated sternly and Tasira nodded.

They moved from guest to guest until they reached the very front of the Hall. Tasira saw the dagger in the top of D'kal's dress and reached down by her breast as she pulled the weapon out.

The face that Tasira made was most amusing, but Seta needed to concentrate on keeping time at a standstill. After the very last guest, even Mara, was disarmed, the two women took their place at the front of the altar. As they let go of their hands, time resumed. A punchbowl shattered in the back of the room and Tasira smiled. D'kal was the first to notice Tasira and Seta at the front of the altar.

Chapter Forty-Seven

"Who are those women! They are defiling the altar of the Priestess," D'kal sounded in a falsely outraged tone. "You men! Go up there and remove them from the bonding ceremony!"

Mara looked at the two women and saw that one of them was Tasira. She turned to Nathan and he nodded that he saw her too. Tasira nodded to them, but said nothing. Nathan and Mara understood, it was important that Tasira say who she was. Seta looked at D'kal.

"Perhaps we should step aside and show this?" She stepped aside to reveal the large pile of weapons. "Is this the altar you think that *we* defile?" Seta said, looking at her hands as if D'kal was of no consequence. D'kal took the insult to heart and grabbed for one of her daggers.

"Are you looking for these? "Tasira asked as she held up all twelve of the weapons that D'kal had brought to the bonding ceremony. "If you can read a room as quickly as I think you can, you should thank the Priestess that we did not kill you." Then Tasira looked at the Elders.

"I believe we were to have a bonding ceremony today, were we not?" Tasira asked Jes. He smiled at her and nodded.

"Yes, young lady. We most definitely were going to have a bonding ceremony." Jes smiled as he answered. He did not know who these two women were, but he knew that they were here to help.

"That is a happy occasion!" Tasira smiled, "And I know how we can assure that it remains that way!" She smiled.

"Aziz, my love, can you join us in the Hall?" Tasira asked loudly. Within a few seconds, she could see her husband making his way through the crowd. There was an audible, collective gasp when they realized he was Xoran. He stood two heads above the average male and a head above her father.

"This is my husband, Aziz. We were bonded about a month ago," Tasira smiled at Aziz lovingly. "Now, we didn't want anything to disturb our bonding ceremony, did we?"

"Absolutely not! I would've become very angry if that had happened." Aziz looked out at the staring crowd. He walked back to his bride's side, speaking directly to her.

"When a Xoran gets enraged, it is twice as bad as the Tuulan Bloodlust, my love. We know exactly what we are doing, we target those who have wronged us and there are often too many dead to count. It is not something you wish to experience," Aziz embellished for the crowd. Tasira kissed him and smiled.

"But we won't have to worry about that happening here. I am sure that no one will disrupt the ceremony." Tasira looked out into the crowd meaningfully. "So, you can just stand here with me Aziz, and we will enjoy the ceremony together, alright?" Tasira looked up at her husband. The look she gave him filled his heart.

"Please continue with the ceremony, Jes. I would like to see these two happy." Tasira finished. Jes nodded and proceeded. They watched as the bonding ceremony took these two young Tuulans and made them one. Everyone was happy and smiling until D'kal spoke up.

"This little game means nothing." D'kal spat at Tasira. "Qata is not my daughter! Let the little boy have her. This bonding does not bind our houses together. That little brat has married a whore that I bought as my house servant," D'kal laughed loudly with a shrill of lunacy. The rest of the spectators gasped at the admission. Tasira looked at her coldly.

"The House of Nathan already knew where she came from. She told them herself." Tasira took a couple of steps toward the Kuutaran. "The difference between you and Qata, is that Qata had no choice." Tasira pointed at D'kal.

"You, on the other hand, chose to be a whore for the riches it would bring to you. I feel sorry for Tavon. He had no idea of the kind of female he chose." D'kal went to scratch the eyes out of Tasira's head until her Aziz stepped in front of her.

"I believe that if you take one more step, I will have a reason to beat you. Choose now, whore." Aziz growled slowly. He wanted her to hear every word he said. D'kal stepped back by her husband Tavon. He stepped sideways from her, making sure that she knew how disgusted he was with her.

"There is still the matter of the right of ascension." D'kal said. "It is time for the issue to be resolved." She pointed at Jes.

"The Council of Nine will have to make a determination. I call for that vote now!" D'kal demanded.

"It is not that easy, D'kal. This is an issue that needs to be researched." Jes stated. D'kal turned on him.

"You just want to keep the power within the Elders. You do not want a Ra Shan because the Elders would be subject to his ruling. It is only about the power, not some type of research that you need to complete. You need no research, old man. You know that the Tuulans and Kuutarans have a shared kinship."

"That half-breed Nathan and his Human wife," D'kal spat on the floor, "They have no right to make decisions for the planet. They are lucky we allow them to live here. You only want to draw this Right of Ascension out longer so that you can find a way to be Ra Shan yourself!" D'kal accused Jes. This caused a flurry of conversation among the people in the Hall. The arguing went on until Seta could take no more.

"That is *enough*!" Seta's voice boomed over the top of the clamoring voices. Tasira looked at Seta and smiled. Seta nodded and turned her attention back to the crowd. "You will address the Council of Nine respectfully or not at all."

Chapter Forty-Eight

"I think I may have a solution to the issue," sounded a voice as clear as a bell. Batah appeared in front of the Statue of the Priestess.

"Will you two, and the Council of Nine, come with me?" They all nodded and followed the floating figure to a wall in the back of the Hall of Elders. There was a painting that covered the wall. It was a replica of the night sky. Eleven pairs of eyes looked at Batah in question. What were they looking at? This painting had been here before any of them had been born. Batah smiled at Tasira.

"Please place your hand over the last star on the right.

As Tasira's hand grew closer the star began to glow. She placed her hand over the star and the wall that had been there disappeared. Behind it was a large half arc. Tasira looked at Batah.

"What is it, Batah?" The visage smiled.

"This is the Archway of the Priestess." Batah smiled."It was used to draw the truth out of a conflict so that the decision would be easier." She motioned to them to bring it out and place it in front of the Statue of the Priestess. Once there, the half arch unfolded until it was a completely solid piece of metal. It was the same black metal that they had all seen used for important items such as the bonding ring Mara wore and the nataks that were used to travel to faraway places.

As the archway became complete, the black metal produced lights that were spaced evenly around the entire half circle. Batah walked up to it and stood directly under it. As she did, she became a whole Tuulan again. Everyone in the Hall stopped speaking.

"My name is Batah. I was the last Supreme Priestess who joined with the planet Tuulani. There have been others after me, but they were not compatible with the Commencement of the Priestess ceremony. They ruled as Tuulan women only, but they had special gifts which helped them keep the planet alive." Batah stopped for a moment and looked at the large archway.

"The Archway of the Priestess has many purposes. One of them is to determine the bloodline of a potential successor. It can read your lineage and intentions down to the smallest of particles and say with certainty if you are worthy or not." Batah stopped and looked at the crowd.

"I understand that there has been much tension for the Right of Ascension to be Ra Shan. The archway will help you determine what the best choice would be." Batah looked at D'kal. "There would be no need to wait for research. The archway cannot lie." Batah looked at Jes and smiled.

"I will leave the rest up to you," she nodded and disappeared. Jes took Batah's cue and stood in front of the archway.

"We will have each immediate family member of the House of Tavon and the House of Nathan walk through the archway, one at a time. We will start with the House of Tavon. Jes motioned for Tavon to step up to the archway.

"Stand under the archway as you saw Batah do. The archway will do all of the work and give us truthful reading. The Elders will write it down on the official record." He looked at Tavon.

"Please step under the arch," Jes motioned. Tavon stepped under the arch and waited. He could see to lights moving around the half-circle until suddenly they stopped. A female voice announced the results.

"Tavon, head of the House of Tavon, one hundred and three years old, seventy-nine percent Tuulan and twenty-one percent Qur'an. One of two males chosen for the bid to be Ra Shan." Jes told him to walk through to the other side. Then he motioned to D'kal to stand under the arch.

D'kal stood still and watched as the lights examined her. She was smug in her assessment of her lineage and could not wait to hear the archway state it. The archway stopped.

"D'kal, spouse of Tavon, seventy-eight years old, lineage proven back to the ruling class of Kuutarii, ninety percent Kuutaran and ten percent Tuulan." D'kal stepped out of the arch and smiled smugly at Mara. She knew Mara would have nothing but the inferior Human race in her lineage. Jes looked at her and stated that the children of the Houses were not subject to this right of ascension and were not required to step under the arch. D'kal protested, loudly, so Jes motioned for Foro to step into the arch.

"Foro, son of D'kal, eighteen years old, seventy percent Kuutaran and thirty percent Tuulan. This child has no lineage similarities with the head of the House of Tavon." D'kal looked at her son in horror, she was always sure that the boy had been Tavon's. Tavon looked at her and folded his arms. Jes smiled as he motioned to Nathan to stand under the arch.

"Nathan, head of the House of Nathan, fifty-seven years old, fifty percent Tuulan and fifty percent Human. Genetic markers of Kala, archeologist who discovered the glowing stone of Kala. One of two males chosen for the bid of Ra Shan." Nathan raised his eyebrows at this information. Jes motioned to Mara. Mara did not want to be judged under the archway. She already knew what it was going to say, and it would damage Nathan's bid to Ra Shan beyond repair. Jes convinced her that it had to be completed. Mara took a deep breath and stepped under the archway, dreading what would happen next.

The archway spun around her and it was making her dizzy. The light seemed to have weight and it pressed on her until she collapsed. She could hear the peal of laughter coming from D'kal. Nathan ran up to Jes in horror.

"What is wrong, why is the archway hurting her?" He asked the Elder. Jes shook his head and looked wide eyed. Nathan pleaded to the Elder.

"We must get her out of there. I will remove my bid for Ra Shan if you will just get Mara out of there." Nathan moved close to the archway and it threw a charge of electricity at him knocking him back. As he got up and was ready to try again, the female voice began to speak.

"Kaana, daughter of the fifteenth Priestess, heir to the position of Priestess, six hundred and two years old," the archway paused momentarily. "Unable to balance the information. Fifty percent Human and fifty percent Tuulan." Mara thought a minute and remembered the name Kaana.

"Tamara go to the house and get the papers from the locked box that Grandfather left me. Hurry!"

Chapter Forty-Nine

Mara sat under the Archway and waited. The female voice was trying to make sense of the error that was made. Soon Tamara came back with the box. Mara spoke slowly to Tamara.

"Find the paper with the old Tuulan writing on it. The one that no one could read." Tamara rifled though the documents until she found it.

"Here it is mother, let me bring it to you." Mara held her hand out.

"No," she yelled, "the archway will not let you come close to me." Tammy looked at her mother, completely helpless to do anything. Mara looked at Tasira.

"I think it is time for you to introduce yourself," She smiled at her smallest child. "You must read the paper. I know that you must possess the knowledge of the old language. Please read it aloud, so we all can understand." Mara finished. Tasira nodded and started to read the document aloud.

"Dear Mara,

When you read this letter, I know you are back on Tuulani. It is the only way for you to understand the writing since it is taught only to a select few. It is the original language of the Tuulans. I know that there may be some confusion when you arrive on my home world, since you do not appear to be Tuulan. Your body will struggle with the pull of Tuulani's need to have a Priestess. It will divide your emotions and you will feel strange, but this feeling will pass when you enter the Archway.

Unfortunately, there are some on Tuulani that may think you are inferior because of your Humanity. They may make your life difficult until your true heritage is revealed.

The Archway will be unable to tell your lineage as I helped your mother to become pregnant with you. I saved the last of my ovules for this purpose. The ovule has the genetic markers from all of the females in my family, so the child born of it will have traits that will be extraordinary.

The child will be mine, your mother's and your father's. You are a very special child and will become the mother and teacher of many children who will make Tuulani whole again. You will have daughters and sons who will each have their own skills, but there will be one that will become even more.

Please give the small piece of metal that is enclosed in this letter to the highest Elder in the Hall of Elders. Only he can place it in the Archway when you go under its scrutiny. Without it, you will be trapped. I love you, Mara. Be Well."

Kaana

Tasira walked over to Jes and handed him the delicate piece of metal. He walked toward the archway and expected to be punished for coming to close. Instead the female voice stopped and said, "Please bring the sample to the archway and place it in the top center stone. There will be a small slot where you will place the sample for analysis."

Jes did as the archway told him and then stepped back. He saw the light change colors and then move around in the same pattern as they did during the first examination. The lights did not have any feel to them at all this time. Mara stood up and the lights stopped moving.

"Mara, daughter of Kaana, sixteenth Priestess of Tuulani, two-hundred and thirty-two years old, fifty percent Tuulan and fifty percent Human. Human lineage back to Nathan Westin, savior of the Tuulans of

Earth." And with that, Mara stumbled out of the archway into Nathan's arms.

"May I go next?" Tasira asked Jes. Jes nodded and helped the young girl into the archway.

"Tasira, daughter of the House of Nathan, direct descendent of Kaana and Kala, trained in the arts of the Daughter of the Priestess, Keeper of the Heart of Tuulani, selected candidate as the future corporeal Priestess of Tuulani, age nineteen years, Seventy five percent Tuulan and twenty-five percent Human. Human lineage back to Nathan Westin, savior of the Tuulans of Earth. Currently pregnant." The female voice stopped.

Tasira looked at Aziz and covered her mouth in surprise. He smiled at his wife and went to her side. Tasira motioned for Seta to come into the archway. Tasira knew Seta didn't want to have all of her lineage told to everyone, because she had no idea of who or what she was. But, reluctantly, Seta gave in to Tasira and stepped into the archway.

"Seta, daughter of Priestess Setari, the Keeper of Light. One hundred percent Tuulan. Heiress of the Keeper of Light, trained in the arts of the Daughter of the Priestess. Future Supreme Priestess of Tuulani, if the oath is accepted." Seta walked out in a daze. How could this be? There were so many different races at the village who had never known their mother or father. It was nearly impossible to be one hundred percent Tuulan in this century. How could this be true? There had been no Priestess for hundreds of years and no Supreme Priestess since the Priestess Batah. Seta looked at the statue of Batah. She pushed the blue jewel in her belt and within seconds Batah appeared in front of her.

"It is true, Seta. You are the next Supreme Priestess of Tuulani. There is one last thing you must consider before you go any further." Batah looked at her and stepped into the archway, allowing her to become flesh and blood once more.

"You will need to give yourself to Tuulani to help it repair. You will no longer have a life as a mortal. You will be the air, the water, the fire and the ground. You will only be able to become flesh and blood within the confines of this archway. Tasira will be the hand that will rule the Tuulans and you will be tempest and calm that will rule the planet itself." Batah reached for Seta and touched her hand.

"Your mother, Setari, had the child she carried placed in a suspended state until the turmoil of Tuulani had passed. She was the first child who would be born from an artificial womb.

Setari had devoted followers who cared for the child and ensured her delivery into the right time. Dela was the last of the followers. She brought you to the village to ensure your safety. She could not tell you or anyone else who you were."

"She waited and watched for the signs that would be presented to her at the right time. She knew that there was another that was coming, and that you and she would bring Tuulani back to a state of peace and great plenty." Batah looked over at Tasira.

"When Tasira was able to open the staircase, I knew my greatest wish had come true. I taught her enough to lead her to you, but the rest you and she had to find out on your own." Batah looked skyward, and then looked at both of the young women.

"In one short cycle of the suns, you must decide if you agree to this calling. It is not an easy decision. You will give up much, but I promise, you will gain even more. Just call for me and I will help you complete the ritual of The Commencement of the Priestess." After those words were said, Batah disappeared once again. Seta walked over to Tasira.

"My mother wanted me. She *didn't* throw me away. She saved me. She wanted me to be born and she wanted us to become friends. She must have had the gift of prophecy." Seta looked at Tasira, and fell to her knees.

"She wanted me, Tasira. I wasn't some mistake that needed to be hidden away." Seta began crying and Tasira knelt down to her.

"We will go to my home and you can rest there in peace." Tasira put a finger under Seta's chin and lifted her face, "It seems that you and I are going to be together for a long time." Tasira smiled and Seta laughed a little. D'kal was not to be denied. She walked up to Tasira and Seta with a wild determined look.

"You are not going to be ruling anything! The Ra Shan will be chosen before you can take your thrones! I will make sure of that!" D'kal screamed and raised her hand. Her hair fell down as she pulled the last dagger in her possession out of her upswept hair. Tasira and Seta had missed one. The Kuutaran threw herself at Seta, bringing down the dagger toward her chest. Tasira watched the action as if time had been slowed, threw herself over Seta, and thrust her hands up to protect herself.

D'kal went flying backwards through the air. Tasira had not touched her, but had concentrated on saving her friend and her own life. D'kal flew toward the wall on the opposite side of the Hall. She hit with a thud and fell down the wall in a heap of fabric and uncoiled hair. Foro screamed and ran to his mother.

"Father, she is still alive!" Foro yelled to Tavon. Tavon looked at the boy and his mother, snorted, turned his back and walked away. Foro was not his and D'kal would no longer be his wife after this evening. He would talk to the Elders to assist him in removing the bonding from his life. He wanted no more from her or her brat. He would spend the rest of his life trying to help the city flourish. He had the wealth if nothing else.

Nathan walked over to D'kal and looked at her. He motioned for the Elder's doctor to come over and assist her. As the doctor came over, so did the male who was in charge of those who had suffered from the Bloodlust.

It had been a very long time since men like Gu'al had been needed, but this evening he placed the chains on D'kal and threw her over his shoulder. She would be the first guest he had 'entertained' at the holding cells. He took the boy, Foro, by the hand and pulled him along. Tavon had no interest in the boy any longer and Gu'al did not blame him. Foro was part of the deceit his mother had perpetrated. Tasira watched the three leave and wondered what would become of the young male.

Chapter Fifty

The entire House of Nathan and the fifty-plus guests arrived at the large home. Each guest was given a meal and a place to sleep. When everyone was settled into a bedroom, the immediate family met in the Great Hall for a discussion of where Tasira had been and what she had been doing since she first went missing. The story finished shortly before the bonding ceremony of Tasira and Aziz.

"Father, I would like you to meet my husband, Aziz." Tasira said with pride showing on her face. Nathan looked at Aziz and walked around him as if he were sizing him up.

"So, you have bonded with our Tasira?" Nathan asked and rubbed his chin as if in thought. Aziz nodded. "And you completed this without the consent of her parents?" Nathan asked, his voice raising a little." Aziz nodded again.

"Yes, I did bond with your daughter. We did not know that we would be reunited with her family." He looked at Tasira and smiled, "I could not say no to her. She had become the center of my life, bit by bit, since I first saw her." Aziz smiled at Nathan. Nathan smiled and nodded his head.

"The females in this family have that effect on men without even trying," Nathan laughed and put his hand on the Xoran's shoulder. Aziz looked at Tasira's father. Tasira had been correct. Her father was much bigger than other Tuulans and her mother was a little smaller than Tasira. He was not going to be different from anyone else in this family. He belonged somewhere. Finally. Nathan then shifted his focus on Seta. Her life would be forever linked with his daughter's. He needed to know what Seta had decided.

"Seta, I understand that you and Tasira have completed training as the Daughter of the Priestess." Nathan looked at her, first with question and then a bit harsher.

"How did this training happen? Did you know that you were training to become a Priestess?" He fired off the questions rapidly and Seta was a little startled. She looked at Tasira in a plea for assistance. Tasira looked at her father sternly.

"Father! Seta is my friend and there is no reason to treat her like the enemy." Tasira stared at her father with her hands on her hips and her foot tapping impatiently. "Ask me the questions and I will tell you all that you need to know!"

Nathan stared at his smallest daughter and was amazed to see the determination in her eyes. Tasira had certainly grown since he last saw her. She had gone from a small, scared young child to a confident young woman who would take a stand for what she believed in. She definitely had gotten that from her mother. He looked at his daughter and her words finally registered, turning his admiration into anger.

"All I need to know?!" Nathan yelled at Tasira. "You had better tell me everything, little one, not just what *you* think I should know!" Nathan was breathing heavily as he stepped in front of Tasira. Tasira stood her ground, she even took a step forward, tipping her head back to look her father directly in the eyes.

"Since you are obviously too emotional to have a conversation, I will tell you a story. It is the story of why I left on my journey and how Seta and I came back to the city. It will give you the answers you need. This is the best I can do for you, Father." Tasira nodded at Nathan and he gave a terse, slight nod back. Mara fought back a smile as her daughter controlled the conversation and made Nathan calm down. Her littlest child had matured into a woman in the time she was gone.

Tasira recited the events of finding the library in the old wing of the house, her travels on the burning sands of the Outlands, and continued through to when she and Seta were trained by the library in the village.

"This was the training for the Daughter of the Priestess." Tasira stopped and looked at the large group in the House of Nathan. "Seta and I didn't understand why we changed each time we entered the chamber, but we knew it was to help Tuulani become whole again." She looked up at her parents.

"There are other villages in the sands that have flourished. Their numbers are few and they are now dying because they have limited resources. The water has diminished, the food is scarce, and most will perish within one generation." Tasira looked at Seta. Seta nodded in agreement to continue.

"These are the descendants of the unwanted children. The ones thrown into the Outlands to die. Unwanted because they had some flaw, real or not, and considered unworthy of being a Tuulan." Tasira paused a moment to slow her breathing and cool her temper.

"Because they were not part of the genetic manipulation that gave the rest of Tuulani only sons, their bloodline is unpolluted. Their females have been having both male and female children as it always should have been. They are the future of Tuulani, and we must save them." Tasira looked at her father and Aziz.

"I know we have only just returned, but Seta and I need to speak privately." Nathan moved as if he was going to go after the two young women, but Aziz grabbed his arm. He looked at Nathan and shook his head. Nathan nodded and brought the remaining family into the Great Hall to wait for the two women to return. Caleb went to the kitchen to get a small snack and drinks for the group with Tinku following closely behind, wagging his tail.

Seta looked at Tasira as she walked into the small room. She could see that they both had the same concerns and that they were the only ones who could make the decision.

"Seta, what knowledge do you have that I may share with you?" Tasira looked at her friend. "What does the Commencement of the Priestess mean? What will happen to you if you decide to accept?"

"I will no longer be the same female you see now." Seta looked at the floor. "I will no longer walk beside you. I will walk with you in spirit only."

"Do you mean that it will be as though you have travelled through the veil?" Tasira asked anxiously. Seta smiled.

"No, not at all. I will be able to see you if you need me by appearing in the archway. I will also be able to project myself just as Batah does." Seta paused. "It's just that things will be different. We will still be friends and help one another, just not as regular Tuulans." Tasira smiled at her friend.

"Since when have we been like normal Tuulans? I was seen as too small and weak to be normal. I doubt that any male in this city would have ever bonded with me." Tasira looked over at Seta. "And you thought that you had been thrown away to live in Mabray. You never knew how important you were until tonight."

"So what shall we do, my not-so-normal friend?" Seta asked with a smile. "Shall we take on this challenge? You will have to be in charge of the Tuulans, settling their fights and squabbles with the help of the Elders. I feel like I am getting the better half of the deal. I get to control the planet and make Tuulani blossom again."

"Will that be enough for you, or will you miss loving someone?" Tasira looked at Seta again, sad that she would be giving up her life here for an unknown.

"Tasira, I had a mate that I loved. When he died, I knew I would never allow myself to go through that pain again." Seta cupped Tasira's chin, lovingly.

"And, I will have you. We are like sisters. Squabbling, loving each other and protecting one other. I will still have that. There is one thing that you do not know that I must share with you." Seta wasn't sure how to phrase her next words.

"If we take this oath, we will age much slower than anyone else. Since you are bonded to Aziz, this will also be true for him and your children. Each generation's effect will lessen a bit, but your life will be long and happy with Aziz." Seta looked up at Tasira.

"The last thing I learned about becoming a Priestess was this, 'Life holds no guarantees, but we can guarantee life for this planet'." Tasira smiled at her.

"I see no reason to decline our responsibility, do you Seta?"

"No. I can see desperate reasons to accept though. I want to do this Tasira, but only if you are with me." Seta looked at her beseechingly. "I will need your strength to make a difference."

"Then we shall do this together." Tasira hugged Seta. It was going to be difficult, but the city and the planet needed them. Their family would grow to understand, she was sure.

"Shall we go back to the Great Hall and tell our family?"

"Our family?" Seta asked, confused. Tasira laughed out loud.

"Didn't I warn you that once you have been accepted by the family, you are one of the family. Like it or not." Tasira walked away giggling. Seta was very glad she had met this young woman.

"Family. I like the sound of that." Seta thought as she too began to giggle.

Chapter Fifty-One

The previous evening had held its challenges. There was yelling and crying and all kinds of emotions crammed into a few hours. As the suns rose, the House of Nathan went to the House of Elders to speak about Seta and Tasira's decision. As they explained it to the Elders, Jes began to smile.

"I am so fortunate to be in the presence of not one, but *two* Priestesses. This is something that has never happened on Tuulani. There has only been one Priestess ruling at a time. I do not understand, but I am grateful," Jes finished. As Jes sat down, Batah appeared in front of the group and began to speak.

"You are right, Jes. There have never been two priestesses ruling at one time," Batah went over to the statue. "Do you see the metal decoration at the base of the statue?" Jes nodded. He had seen it before, but had never given it more than a passing glance. It was only decoration as far as he knew.

"I want you to go over with Seta and Tasira and open the metal drawer." Jes looked at the two women and went over to the metal plaque that held Batah's name.

"Alright, now what do we do?" Jes asked. Batah looked at the two women.

"Tasira, Seta," Batah began, "I want you to hold hands as you did last night. The rest of the Tuulans in the room will not know that time has passed. Time will stop." The two women nodded in understanding.

"When your hands have clasped, the drawer will open. There will be a piece of Hermes paper inside. Retrieve it, and the drawer will close. Drop your hands and give the paper to Jes when this is complete." Jes nodded and the two did as they were told. When the task was completed, they dropped hands.

"When will you start?" Jes asked and then looked at the paper. "The task is complete?" Tasira nodded and handed the paper to Jes. It took a while to read the old writing through squinted eyes for the ink was faded and difficult to see. When he was through, he placed the paper down on the table where he had sat with the other

Elders. Nathan was getting a little impatient with this, but it was Aziz who spoke first.

"What does the paper say, Jes?" Aziz asked impatiently. Jes looked up at him. He didn't know how to explain this, but he would give it a try.

"Tuulani has only had one priestess at a time. When the planet started its' downward progression, we had war, genocide, famine, loss of resources. And death. The last Priestess was Kaana." He closed his eyes and sighed.

"She went in search of a place where the Tuulans could find unpolluted genetic material. Many followed, but others, believing that the Earth was inferior, chose to go to other planets. Most of those quests ended in death." Tears welled in the old Tuulan's eyes.

"The majority of survivors on Earth were systematically hunted and murdered. But Kaana knew that she had created a child who would usher in a new life for Tuulani. That life came in three parts. The first part was the birth of Tasira. The second was the trip back to Tuulani, and Tasira's quest into the Outlands where she met Seta. Tasira needed to find her own way, and Batah helped her do that." Jes looked up at Tasira and Seta.

"But Tasira did not have all of the knowledge she needed, did she, Jes?" Seta asked. The old Tuulan shook his head 'no'.

"The third part of the new life would be Seta and Tasira's commencement and the systematic cleansing of the planet. No single Priestess would be able to do this on her own. That is why we have two Priestesses," Jes paused.

"Seta you are the one who will change the planet. Not all change is pleasant. It will be as if Tuulani is being reborn. We will experience hardship at first and some of us may die, but the ultimate outcome will be that our planet and our race will survive." Jes looked at Seta again.

"You will have to destroy some things in order to rebuild others." Seta gave a nod. His face turned to Tasira.

"Tasira, you will have to keep the Tuulans strong. There will be those who will try to kill you. If they succeed, we will all perish and Seta will be alone forever." Tears were now running down the old Tuulan's face as he finished the announcement. "You had to know these things in order to make your decision. I will show you to my room where you may talk it over."

Seta and Tasira looked at each other, they had already spoken it over with their family. One last glance at Aziz and Tasira knew that he would be with her no matter what her decision. Tasira and Seta spoke in one voice.

"We have made our decision and we wish to complete the commencement and fulfill our responsibility." Jes smiled at them and the others. Batah appeared once more.

"We will prepare the Commencement of the Priestess ceremony. We will convene at the Altar of the Priestess at sundown." With that said Batah disappeared and the group went back to the House of Nathan.

The remainder of the day was spent introducing Seta to her now very large family. Tasira played with the twins, and the two young women prepared for the evening. It was an eventful, happy and yet sobering day.

Batah had sent a message from the House of Elders that there were garments being prepared for Seta and Tasira. They were given a plain sheath to cover themselves, and were to walk through the city, barefoot, to the House of Elders. There, they were to be received by the eldest women in the city. The remaining preparations would be completed at that time, and the family would not see them again until they were presented at the altar.

Seta went to the room she had been given and contemplated the life ahead of her. She had asked for a number of sheets of Hermes paper and was now writing down everything she was told in her training. These documents were to be hidden away where no one, but she, would know of their existence.

Tasira saw that her father was sitting at the head of the table in the Great Hall with Aziz, discussing something of importance. She walked up to the table and both men smiled at her. Her father looked very proud of her and yet somehow sad.

"Father, you look sad." She looked at him with a patient empathy. "Don't worry about the commencement and what it means. Think more about how you can make every moment matter. I will be in the city with you every day. We will see more of each other than ever, and you will get to see your first grandchild born here on your home planet. He or she will take up yours and Mother's time I'm sure." Tasira went over and hugged Nathan. Her father hugged her so hard she didn't think he was ever going to let go. When Nathan was through, he stepped back and held her arms.

"I think we are all fortunate that you came into our lives. You were the last one of the triplets born, did you know that?" Tasira nodded at her father with shining eyes.

"You were the smallest and the quietest of all of your siblings, but your mother knew right away that you were special." A tear rolled down Nathan's cheek.

"And when I thought your mother was lost to me, you were the one who reminded me of her most." He hugged her again and then cleared his throat.

"I'll leave you and Aziz alone. I am sure there are many things that you need to discuss." He walked out of the room and shut the door behind him. Tasira watched him for a moment and then looked at her husband with tears in her eyes. Aziz smiled with a bit of sadness in his eyes.

"He is very proud of you, but he is as scared as I am about losing you." Aziz looked down at the wooden floor.

"You will change, you know. There is no other way to become a Priestess. You *are* the change that will come. You and Seta will control this planet and that will require your time." Aziz looked up at her.

"I know that we will have little time together, but I will always be there, waiting." As he reached over to kiss her, he took something out of his pocket. He knelt down on both knees and looked at her.

"Your father told me the story of how he knew that your mother loved him." Aziz held up a small box. "This box holds a ring that will bind with your finger. It is a final step in being bonded to me." Tasira could see the anxiety in his eyes as he looked at her.

"Once you place this ring on your finger, no one will be able to take it off, not even you. By placing it on your finger, you are declaring that you love me and want to be with me forever. There is no way to take away the bonding once this is done." Aziz handed her the box and stood up. "I will leave you now to think of what your answer will be." He turned and headed towards the door."

"It fits quite nicely." Tasira said nonchalantly. "I think..." she could not finish. Aziz had already gathered her up and was kissing her. She started to laugh and tipped her head back to laugh harder.

"Did you really think I would say no?" She giggled once more and then looked at the man who held her two feet in the air. "I told you once before, it is very difficult to get away from one of the women in my family once she has her heart set on being your mate. You were doomed the first moment I saw you, carrying me in your arms to the village." Aziz's brow ridge raised a bit. "Oh yes, Aziz. I figured that one out too." Tasira smiled broadly at him. The smile melted into a smoky look. Aziz set her down and she grabbed his hand and led him to their bedroom. Tasira had to hurry afterwards to take another bath to be ready for the commencement.

Chapter Fifty-Two

Seta and Tasira walked shoulder to shoulder through the city, barefoot. They had nothing but a simple dress to cover them along their way. Every citizen in the city came out and lined the path that they would have to take. Not a single sound was made. No speaking, just a respectful look as they went by.

They finally reached the Hall of Elders and waited in front of the large doors. A group of women came outside, split into two groups and each one led one of the women away. Seta and Tasira looked over their shoulders at one another and smiled. They knew they would be seeing each other soon.

When the suns had set, the remaining member of the House of Nathan walked up to the House of Elders as well. A young man told them that the courtyard overlooking the cliffs is where the ceremony would be held.

"Outdoors?" Nathan looked at Mara and Aziz. "The commencement was to be held at the Altar of the Priestess. Where are we going now?" Aziz shrugged and went to the edge of the city where the courtyard was located. When they arrived, they were ushered up to the front of the crowd, where seats were arranged for them. The courtyard was decorated with plants, and small lamps flamed in a semicircle. The very center of the courtyard held a single water fountain which filtered down into a large glass bowl.

The Elders walked onto the courtyard in a single line. Jes waited for each of them to be seated and then he walked up to the fountain. He motioned for two men to roll the Archway of the Priestess towards him until he was under it.

"Batah, we call on you to complete the Commencement of the Priestess." Jes returned to his seat and Batah spoke to gathering.

"Seta and Tasira. Please come to me and stand in front of these witnesses." A loud rumbling sound came from below the crowd and the concentric circle pattern on the courtyard opened up. An oval platform came to the surface and presented Seta and Tasira to all who attended. Seta was dressed in an iridescent silver dress that sparkled like stars. Her hair was curled, ribbons flowing and a silver paint on her eyes.

Tasira stood on the opposite end of the oval. She was dressed in a deep red dress that was belted under her breasts with heart shaped jewels. Tasira's hair was simply braided with a red ribbon that shone brightly in her ebony hair. Her lips had been lightly touched with a red stain and a glossy finish. Both women were entrancing in their own unique way.

"Seta and Tasira have been chosen by Tuulani to lead you and help you repair the damage that was inflicted upon her. The transition will be difficult, but the result will bring forth a thriving Tuulan planet and culture. This is how it was meant to be from the start."

"Seta will rule the elements, and Tasira, the heart of the planet. Both women have agreed to take on this responsibility and are prepared to make any sacrifice needed of them. They will serve you well if you support and respect them. This is not about power, but about survival. They will give you this, and more, if you honor them." Batah motioned to them. "Seta and Tasira, you must choose a male to assist you in the unfolding." Both women nodded.

"I will choose my husband, Aziz, to assist me," Tasira stated formally. She looked to Seta for her choice.

Tasira was not quite sure who she would choose. She knew that Seta felt all alone. Seta smiled at her, knowing that Tasira was worried about her.

"I will choose my adoptive father, Nathan, to assist me." Seta stated, smiling. Batah nodded and motioned to Jes to retrieve the males that had been chosen. Each man was instructed to stand next to the woman who had called his name. As they complied, Batah moved in front of the archway.

"Aziz, Nathan. You must reach to the top of the arch and find the latch that holds the two sides together. When you have found it, unlatch it and carefully lay your side of the arch down on the ground." She looked at them again.

"When the Arch lay flat, assist each woman as she steps inside the oval. Afterward, you will sit next to the Elders.

Nathan and Aziz felt on top of the arch until Aziz found the latch. He tapped Nathan's hand and looked at him. Nathan nodded and soon the arch split open. When they were done, Aziz helped Tasira step inside the oval and Nathan did the same with Seta. Once the entire ceremony was completed, Batah stood in front of the oval.

"A Priestess has the right to name her city but this is an unusual set of circumstances. We have two Priestesses. One is no more important than the other, so I have asked Tasira and Seta to find a name that would please them both." Tasira nodded at Seta.

"We name our city B'hest Tuulani. It means 'Paradise of Tuulani'." Tasira could see the name was being accepted by the citizens and she was glad. It had long been a point of argument amongst the city residents and was one issue that would no longer be contested. Batah nodded to Tasira and Seta. She turned around and rose above them, spinning over the cliff, hanging in mid air.

"Tasira, Seta...please join your hands." Batah instructed. "Once the Commencement is completed, I will finally rest," the visage smiled at them.

"I want you to know I am proud of you. Without your courage, the planet would've been sentenced to die." Batah looked at the young women who were holding hands.

"Say the words you've memorized. Your pledges are very different, but they will bond you together as if you had been born twins. Each will know the other's thoughts, and you will work as one to save Tuulani." Batah paused.

"I will slowly fade away until I have been replaced by you, Seta. That is when you will know that the Commencement is almost complete. Start now and do not stop until the transition is finished."

Tasira and Seta glanced at each other and started their individual incantations. As they continued, the words seem to blend into one voice that spoke a language that had never been heard before. They rose up from the ground and started spinning in a circle. Batah watched and with each slow rotation of the women, her appearance became less visible.

Chapter Fifty-Three

The spinning increased in speed until Tasira and Seta lost their grip on one another. Seta reeled backward and stopped above the deep gorge outside of the city.

Tasira stopped above the courtyard. The ground beneath the oval fell away to reveal a tunnel below. The incantations continued, making each woman spin individually above the place where she had been thrown.

Seta became more transparent as a large funnel of sand formed and moved closer to the courtyard. Whispers of fear began. A new sense of anxiety overcame the crowd. They watched as clouds formed over the top of the funnel.

As the sky continued to darken, the funnel moved into the Outlands, and suddenly fell to the ground in one large mass. The clouds moved around Seta, forming a cocoon. Soon her defined figure become more transparent, until the spinning stopped and a rainstorm began. All traces of Seta's physical form were gone.

The Tuulans stared at the sky, unbelieving, and held their arms upward. It was the first time most of them had seen rain. The city had been surviving on the diminishing aquafers below.

Now, there were small gullies of water running between the dunes in the Outlands. The wall of sand that had kept them separated from the rest of the planet had disappeared and the expansive desert was no longer hidden from their view.

The suddenness of the changes the Commencement brought a sweeping panic. The terror increased until many of the citizens were running for the shelter of their homes.

Tasira turned upright and floated over the tunnel that appeared to go into the center of Tuulani. She looked at the crowd and floated to the courtyard edge where she daintily stepped onto the dais that stood at the edge of the ovals.

"There is no reason to run." Tasira said. Her voice was soft, but it echoed as if it had been magnified a hundred times. The crowd stopped and turned around to look at the small figure standing in the center of the courtyard.

"Return to me and I will tell you of the changes that are yet to come." The group came back to listen to their new Priestess. She had a way about her that commanded authority.

"The rain will continue until fertile ground beneath the sands can emerge again. I will take the washed sands and give them to Seta. She will form them into a mountain to remind us of how fortunate we are to have our planet back. It will be visible for hundreds of miles and will serve as a landmark to our city." Tasira looked at the crowd.

"You will need to work the soil, as our ancestors did, to multiply the harvests. There will be something for every house to contribute to our success." Tasira smiled at the crowd.

"We must work together as one race, and with one purpose. To undo the damage our ancestors forced upon our planet. Seta has sacrificed herself to help us with our recovery."

"Now, you must decide how much you are willing to give. Without your help, Tuulani...and Seta, will die within one or two generations." Tasira looked at the crowd once more.

"Go to your homes and think about what you are willing to give. What will you be willing to sacrifice? I will begin receiving citizens in one week. We will work side by side to make our children's futures better."

Aziz watched as his young wife stepped towards him. She looked at the departing crowd and smiled at him. As he smiled back, she took one more step towards him and collapsed onto the floor of the courtyard. Her hair and dress folded around her, obscuring his view of her face.

"Tasira!" Aziz ran to her and folded her in his arms. "I will take you home." He looked at Nathan and Mara with worried eyes, "You need to rest and gain your strength. I will bring you to Pel." He continued speaking to Tasira as if she were awake and able to hear his every word. Aziz ran towards The House of Nathan with his wife in his arms. Nathan watched as the hulking body ran faster than anyone or anything he had seen before. Mara touched Nathan's arm.

"She will be alright." She looked up at Nathan and smiled. "She is a Priestess now. Seta will protect her mind and body, and Aziz will soothe her heart and soul. Until last evening, we had thought Tasira was dead." Mara smiled up at Nathan.

"Poor Aziz. He has gotten more from their bonding than he could've imagined." Nathan smiled back at her.

"Just wait until their children are born." Nathan said, smiling. Mara just looked at him and started laughing. They continued to walk toward their home to see what had become of Tasira.

Chapter Fifty-Four

A large figure crossed through the dark doorway from the main cellhouse. The figure was carrying a body with flowing hair and pulling a smaller figure, in chains, behind him.

The hidden wing had once housed violent Tuulans, but now stood forgotten and empty. Most had no knowledge of its' history... or its existence.

As a large hand closed the door, the faint sound of a scream was silenced.

Made in the USA
Monee, IL
15 June 2023